WHEN LOVE CALLS

LILLIANNE LONG

WESTBOW°
PRESS
A DIVISION OF THOMAS NELSON
& ZONDERVAN

WestBow Press books may be ordered through
booksellers or by contacting:

WestBow Press
A Division of Thomas Nelson & Zondervan
1663 Liberty Drive
Bloomington, IN 47403
www.westbowpress.com
1 (866) 928-1240

ISBN: 978-1-4908-6964-3 (sc)

Library of Congress Control Number: 2015902146

Print information available on the last page..

WestBow Press rev. date: 03/24/2015

CHAPTER I

"Loro!" The voice came from above me, and I froze. Looking up at the cliffs, I could see the figure of a man on horseback silhouetted against the sky. I looked around me. There was no one there but me. Below me, the sea crashed onto black rocks, with just a small beach behind the rocks guarding the place under the cliffs where I sat.

"Get away from there. You know better than that," the silhouette called angrily. I sat up slowly. I had been sunbathing as I sketched in the fantastically beautifully place, and I had thought I was alone.

"I beg your pardon. Are you speaking to me?"

"What? You know I'm speaking to you. What a silly, sullen wench you are sometimes, Loro. Get away from there. You know it's dangerous. Get out of there. Or do I have to come down and get you out?" The words did not make sense. I did not know this man. I didn't know anyone in Santa Barbara or Carpentaria. I had arrived in town just two days ago on a Greyhound bus with a small, blue suitcase containing only a few changes of clothing. The day

1

before yesterday I had paid a week's rent on a small motel apartment, and I had three hundred dollars left out of the money I had brought with me. Yesterday morning I had eaten breakfast at a coffee shop in a drugstore at a mall, which resembled a Spanish plaza. And I had taken the bus to Carpentaria.

It had not been hard to find the Fuente estate. Mom had told me to look for two iron gates off Highway 101, with a fountain set back from the arched entry way. I took a taxi and found it easily.

However, I had not entered those imposing gates. Instead, I had stopped across the highway from them, out of traffic, and stared for a long time. Then I returned to my motel room. There I had spent the remainder of the day staring blindly at a TV set and chewing my nails. Last night I had decided to return to Alabama.

Awakening early, however, and after I had read the Book, prayed and thought for awhile, I squared my shoulders and decided it was something I must do. I would never respect myself again if I did not try. If I tried and failed—well, I would face that if it occurred.

But my second trip was no more successful than the first. Again, I stood staring at the beautiful villa. And then, delaying any decision, found my way down to the beach where I slowly gathered my things—sketchbook, watercolors—still glancing up at the man silhouetted above me against the light. He had dismounted and was shouting, in Spanish, and had begun to climb down the cliff toward me. As he neared, he returned to English.

"Loro, have you lost your mind? Of all the stupid…you could be killed! Don't you ever think?" He was jumping from a large rock toward my space, about fifteen feet above the beach.

Suddenly there was a rumble and I felt the ground beneath my feet tremble. The man jumped, caught me around the waist before I could move, and jumped again toward the beach below. The rumbling intensified behind us, and I felt my legs and feet being buried. A large boulder, two feet across came to rest gently beside our heads.

He had partially covered me with his body. Slowly he moved and sat up.

"Loro, what in the blazes! You know that cliff is not safe. It's been crumbling for years. Whatever possessed you?" His fear was taking the form of anger and he was taking the anger out on me. He brushed hard at a pair of cleaned and pressed but now dusty blue jeans removed a boot and emptied dirt from it.

I began to pull myself together and sat up, retrieving my work from underneath a pile of dirt, and glanced at it ruefully. It was ruined.

"It seemed safe enough until you got here."

"I was a fool for coming down, I know. But you just sat there staring at me and not moving!" He removed the other boot and shook it. Replaced it. Then stood up, and taking my hands, pulled me to my feet. "All right?"

Everything felt all right until I tried to put my weight on my right foot. "Let me sit down a minute."

With his help, I eased down on the rock, rubbed my foot, and then looked up at him. I really had not had a chance to look at him, or him at me. He had been a dark shape against the light. Then he had been bent over his boots. I had gotten the impression of a tall man with a strong, compact body when he had leaped from that rock and plucked me up.

Now I saw before me a face with dark skin, a little too rugged for handsome and a little too handsome for rugged, a hard jaw, narrow, brown, almost black hunter's eyes, and the high check bones and smooth planes of Indian blood.

"But..." he looked into my face, confused. "You're not Loro!"

"Yes, I know that." I rubbed my ankle. "I was trying to tell you, but you were too busy blessing me out."

"What is your name? I could have sworn...you are the image of Loro except for the eyes. Loro's eyes are green. Yours are blue. But the shape is the same! And the hair...now I see that yours is a few shades lighter than Loro's.

I was still rubbing my ankle, but I looked up at him suddenly. "Loro who?"

"Loro de la Fuente. Don't you know you're on Fuente land?"

I digested that, and then shook my head. "I didn't know. I was sketching."

"You don't know Loro? You're not related somehow? I've known Loro for years, and I would have sworn...! The resemblance is remarkable."

"Loro? That's an unusual name."

"Short for Delores."

"Do you go around sweeping this Loro off her feet every time you meet her Mr...?"

"Casabon. Ron Casabon. You should not have been here. That cliff is dangerous. It's always crumbling. Someone was killed here...." he abruptly stopped.

"I've been in California two days, Mr. Casabon. I didn't know."

"Your voice is like Loro's, but the accent is different. I hear it now. The South is in your voice. Georgia? Louisiana?"

I shook my head. "Alabama,"

"No, you wouldn't have known. Look at that." He nodded toward the pile of rubble behind us. "You might have been buried under five tons of rocks and mud right now."

I looked and shuddered, realized he was right. "Did I say thank you? I'm afraid not. Well, thank you. It's deceptive, isn't it?"

"Yes. Californians usually stay away from these kinds of cliffs. A lot of people have been buried under these slides."

"It is so beautiful here. The blue-green water, the gold sand, it looks like peace and happiness."

He shrugged. "Beautiful things are often deceptive. Don't they teach you that in Alabama? Here, let's have a look at that ankle."

I extended my leg. The ankle had begun to swell and the side of my foot was puffy. "You're not going to be able to walk on that."

"Maybe I can. Let me try." I stood up and put the foot down tentatively. "Ouch!" I clung to his arm.

"No good." He sat me down on the rock again. "Look, Miss...?"

"Templeton. Gail Templeton."

"Miss Templeton, if you can wait, I'll bring my horse down. Unless he shied when that section of cliff fell, he should be at the top waiting for me. It was only by chance that I was riding this way this morning and saw you here."

He left, walking down the beach, and I saw him turn up the stairs I had descended, evidently the Fuentes' back gate... It must be wonderful to have a private entrance to this paradise, I thought wistfully.

It had been such a short time—two months—since my world had turned upside down. Before that, I had no idea of ever coming here. California had been just a geographical location in my mind—a long, narrow, over-populated state on the far-away West Coast. If I had thought about it at all, it was with curiosity when they told me—what was it my geography teachers had told me? California is a state of extremes—extreme beauty, extreme ugliness. No trees, or the largest trees in the world. Flat desert. High mountains. Waterless, it feeds the nation. Pulitzer Prize winners lived there, and so did the homeless who walked the streets of the large cities mumbling to invisible companions. Politically it was far left and far right. Not many in the middle. Its movie industry had shamelessly exploited, glorified, and promoted the wicked and materialistic. And yet, occasionally burst forth with brilliance, telling of the wonderful and the good. Many of the top stars had gone the way of sin and drugs. Some of them had found God. There are many phony religions there. Yet Christian history had been made there, and some of the most reputable religious organizations in the world call California home. Azua street, in a run down section of Los Angeles had been the birthplace of the Pentecostal-Charismatic movement in 1906. Trinity Broadcasting Network in Santa Ana sends the message of radical Christianity around the world. It had given Corrie Ten Boom, one of the foremost Christians of the last century, a home—the only home she had in her saintly old age. It was a land, in short, where spirits—good and bad—were awake and prevalent. In so much of America the spirits sleep. California is a beacon, a pathfinder—to both the saintly and wicked.

It had been last Christmas that I dug out the birth certificate from the bottom of the trunk in the attic. Some of us teachers had planned to go abroad for summer vacation, and I needed my birth certificate to get a visa. I knew Mom was ill, even then, though I had not realized how ill or I would never have planned on a trip abroad. I wasn't sure where it was, and at the bottom of an old trunk I found, not my adoptive birth certificate—but an old one, which had evidently not been out of the trunk since I had been born.

And there it was--birthplace, Santa Barbara, California.

I had gone to her room. She sat up and looked at me expectantly. "Mom, I didn't know I was born in Santa Barbara. And to someone named Costello?"

She delayed for a long time before she answered. "No, you didn't. Sit down, Gail. I have to tell you something."

She told me then that she and dad were not my birth parents as I had thought. They had adopted me as a baby. My birth mother—Elfrida Costello—was a socialite in Santa Barbara, and my adopted mother was a college friend of hers from Alabama. Elfrida had been a freshman when she got pregnant. My mother, Goldie, had been a graduate student, married to Joseph Templeton, at that time a navy pilot who was stationed at a near-by airbase. Goldie could not have children because of complications, which had necessitated a hysterectomy in her past.

Elfrida was one of those rare Spanish blondes. Her parents, old Mexican aristocracy, had been horrified at the pregnancy. Consequently, because she knew Goldie and Joseph wanted a child so badly, I was given to them. I had a wonderful childhood! God had been good to me, and they were loving, caring parents. Sadly, dad had died a couple of years ago, and my mother had followed him a few months after she had told me the truth about my birth.

Discovering all of this was shocking, and I felt strange. Nevertheless, I should have known something of the sort. All of my life I had the uneasy feeling that I was not exactly like my cousins. Don't get me wrong. I had never been treated differently within my family. They had all accepted me completely. Mom and Dad's relatives were Bible-belt, ice-cream social, porch swing-type Christians, and there are no better people than that. I had always attended school with my cousins. We celebrated the Fourth of July with watermelon, fried chicken and chocolate cake picnics, highlighted by fireworks mostly set off by the men in the family. My cousins and I had attended each other's graduation exercises, and later cheered each other into careers. It was a great childhood, but there were times when I had felt, well, set apart, so to speak. Different.

Once when I was having a childhood spat with my cousin, Rosamund, who was nearest my age, I had lost my temper and hurled a toy across the room at her, missing her, but arousing the ire of her parents.

"Could have been worse," My Uncle Tom, Rosamund's daddy had said, picking up his crying daughter. "Looks like she had pretty good aim. If Rosie hadn't stumbled she'd have gotten a good conk on the head. They're famous for their fiery tempers."

"Hush Tom," my mother had said frantically, looking at me.

"That Spanish blood," my Aunt Nan had said. But she had smiled at me. "You watch it girl. That's hot stuff and might get you in trouble some day."

"Nan, she doesn't..." my mother began. "Just hush, will you!"

"Ok, we'll hush. But you should have told her by now."

"It's just a kid fight. No harm done," my Uncle had said.

Later I had asked my mother about it. "What's Spanish blood, Mama?"

"Well, the Spanish people have a reputation for being quick tempered, Gail. They are quick to love and quick to anger, that's all."

"What were Uncle Tom and Aunt Nan talking about, then?"

9

"They were saying it's like you have Spanish blood, the way you threw that toy at Rosie. You could have hurt her, if you had hit her."

"But I don't hate her."

"Well, you reacted too quickly, before you thought about it, really."

"That's Spanish blood?"

"Something like that."

I was a bright child, all A's in school, and not easily satisfied with lame answers. The Spanish blood incident impressed me enough that I took a couple of Spanish classes in college. Although that, and other little family incidents, told me I was somehow different, and set me apart. I could never find out why.

I went to college and graduated *cum laude*, my degree in special education. Then I went on to receive a Fellowship and secured my Master's Degree. I had been teaching a short time and had a few private clients, loving my work and doing well in it. Then my father died suddenly of an aneurism, and my mother became sick with cancer a few months later. It was almost as though she had been waiting for me to get on my own.

I hadn't thought she was that ill before I found the birth certificate and learned that she was not my birth mother. She told me that Elfrida Castillo had belonged to a family that had once had old money, the extremely wealthy land-grant kind of money that the Spanish in California had at one time. Her ancestors had lived there for generations. She told me that Elfrida had since married, and her name was now Fuente, that she lived with her husband, Jorge on a cliff by the Pacific, and the name of her place was La Fuente—the Fountain. For a few years they had written to each other regularly, exchanging news and pictures, but when Elfrida married she became apprehensive. Worried that her new husband would discover too much. So, by mutual agreement, most of the correspondence had stopped.

Mercifully, my mother's sickness did not last long, and she died only a few months later. That was last fall. Her illness had taken most of her savings, although she had willed the house to me. It was rented now, with my Uncle Tom overseeing it.

I could see him coming back, half a mile down the beach. I know something about horses, and riding. My mother's family were farmers, and climbing on the back of a horse was the first thing the children in the family did after they learned to walk. My summer vacations were spent on the family farm with cousins, planting and harvesting gardens, cooking, cleaning, milking cows, mucking stables, and riding horses through the beautiful Alabama countryside. Some of my cousins rode in competitions, and I developed an eye for good horsemanship. I could see this man was a good rider. He was coming at a moderate gallop. The horse was a buckskin stallion that ran with the level-back natural grace of a thoroughbred. The man sat strong, one with the flowing motion, his torso rocking easily in the saddle. I watched him approach along that beautiful wild beach, he and his buckskin running in the wind, the sunshine's lazy buttery glow gilding sea and sand, and the edges of the black rocks along the cliffs. It was so beautiful. My fingers itched to sketch the scene.

He dismounted, swinging easily from his saddle to the ground before he was fully stopped. "Are you all right?" He looked keenly into my face as I nodded. "Well then, up you go."

I stood hesitantly and he lifted me easily to the rock. Holding on to him, I got my good foot in the stirrup and swung up behind the saddle.

"Looks like you've been on horses before. Good. That eliminates an extra bit of trouble. I wondered if you were going to be one of the scary, screaming types, but I didn't think so." He swung into the saddle in front of me, and without thinking about it, I looped my arms around his waist. His body was solid and warm. Suddenly I realized this was not one of my cousins, and hastily dropped my arms to my sides. "Loro is an expert horsewoman. Strange that you should be so much alike."

"This Loro. Did you say her name was Fuente?"

"Delores de la Fuente"

"Do you know her well?"

"Quite well."

"She is my age?"

"I don't know your age. Loro is eighteen."

I wanted terribly to ask more—if Delores and her mother were presently at home, if there was a way to meet them without bursting in on them unexpectedly. But I decided to keep quiet for the present.

"I shall have to write my family back in Alabama and tell them I have a mysterious twin out here." I said. "Are there other children in this de la Fuente family who may look like me?"

"No. Just Loro. She has a brother, but he takes after the other side of the house. Loro looks like her mother."

My heart began to beat faster. "Her mother?"

"Yes, Elfrida."

"Then Loro is still living with her family? Or is she in college?"

"Finishing high school. She'll go to college next year, if her parents prevail. But she's not very heavy in the intellectual department. Her brain is all right, but she's willful and spoiled. She wants to have a good time and then marry. She's very pretty, and has already had several offers, much to the distress of her parents. I might have courted her myself; she's pretty enough, But she's too young for me. I married someone else."

I said nothing but moved back a little from him.

"My wife is dead," he said abruptly.

"Oh, I'm sorry."

"Happened two years ago…but we were talking about Loro. I imagine her parents' wishes will eventually prevail. She'll go to college, and take her time marrying. She's hard headed and independent, but young ladies with Spanish blood generally are required to listen to their parents."

He evidently decided we were discussing his neighbors too much, then, because he abruptly changed the subject. "What brought you to California, Miss Templeton?"

"I wanted to get out of my small town, see the world. My parents are dead—mother died this past spring. Plus, I'm a teacher, and California pays its teachers well!"

"I noticed you had been sketching, down on the beach. Do you teach art?"

"No. Art is a hobby. My field is special education. I teach exceptional children."

"Extraordinary!"

"Hardly. It's a pretty popular subject these days. A lot of children need help."

"But I mean...Miss Templeton, I hope you will not mind...I'm taking you to my home. It's the next house over." The cliffs had broken to a slope of green grass and he turned off on a path beneath trees, going up an incline. When we breasted the hill there was, before us, a Spanish-type house in stucco and adobe brick. It was not a tall house, but it rambled over a half acre or so of grounds landscaped in bougainvillea and roses.

CHAPTER II

"It's a beautiful house, Mr. Casabon. Is it your family home?"

"No. My family lived across town, and I was raised there in the *barrio*. I built Buenaventura myself." He directed the horse to the front door and swung down easily from the saddle. I slid from the horse as he caught me and placed me gently on the ground.

A dark head and a pair of sparkling dark eyes appeared from around a corner. A boy of about fourteen was tossed the reins, and Ron Casabon said something in Spanish and turned back to me.

"Into the parlor, Miss Templeton."

I clutched his arm and attempted to walk, but my foot was quite swollen now. When I took off my shoe, I could see that the base of each toe was bruised and purple.

"Well," he said, examining it, "we did a good job of it, didn't we? Come inside, Miss Templeton." With that, he lifted me effortlessly and bore me into a beautifully decorated, long, narrow parlor. The walls were a dead, chalk white, the floors wide-planked hardwood, varnished to a rich dark perfection. At one end of the room there was a huge fireplace of adobe brick inlaid with some sort of mosaic. The room was relieved from austerity by touches of deep, clear blues, reds and yellows—primary colors, carrying with them their hints of violent energy.

He sat me down on a black leather sofa covered with a brilliant Indian blanket.

"Welcome to Buenaventura, Miss Templeton."

"It's lovely."

He smiled with pleasure, and it occurred to me that it was the first time I had seen those stern features relax. I knew he didn't smile often, and that was a great pity. It was like the sun breaking upon a cloudy day.

"Too masculine, perhaps. I..."

He stopped, and the smile and the gentleness disappeared from his features, as they lapsed into the rigid austerity that had been there before. A door onto the balcony over one side of the living room was opening, and a child came out. He watched her as she made her way down the stairs and to the long fireplace. She did not look at us nor speak. Seemingly shut in a world of her own, she turned from the fire and went the length of the room, grabbed a sofa pillow and ran with it through a door, disappearing.

"My daughter, Miss Templeton. Tabitha. We call her Tabbie."

"I see." I did see—too much. "She's autistic?"

"Yes."

He gave a great sigh and then looked directly into my eyes. "Miss Templeton, you'll have to forgive me. I have been searching for a private teacher for Tabbie for a month now. It's interesting that you came along at this time. If you have the proper qualifications, would you like a job?"

I stared at him. "Mr. Casabon, you don't know me very well."

"I'm a lawyer, Miss Templeton. I will check your credentials and your references. The fact that you are from Alabama is a mark in your favor. There's something down-home that I like about the southern states, which California does not have. If it could be packaged and shipped, it would sell well! Maybe Tabbie could use that quality. Maybe it's something she needs, part of what is lacking. Whatever it is—we can always hope. They really don't know a great deal about what causes autism, or what can cure it."

"No."

"Maybe it's as simple as a warm heart. I don't know. Anyway, I won't ask for your answer right away, but I'd like to know as soon as you can make a decision."

"Would it be preferable to put her in a special school?"

"Maybe, but I love my daughter and I'd like to keep her with me. And I'm a proud man. I'd rather it would be handled privately."

"Excuse me, Mr. Casabon," I interrupted, "If by 'it' you mean Tabitha...."

He turned a withering stare on me, but I held his gaze, not backing down. "I didn't mean my daughter, Miss Templeton. I mean the matter of this illness is to be kept in my family."

"I see, but illness is illness, Mr. Casabon. There is no reason to be ashamed of it."

"I like your approach, Miss Templeton. However, for other reasons, there has been enough town gossip about my family, and I will not willingly give reason for any more. People are people, and I'm a realist. We would like them to be different, but, too often, they are not. About the position, I'll match the salary paid by the public school system— which, as you mentioned, is a good one in this state. But I'm getting ahead of myself. I haven't asked you about your family. Do you have family here in California?"

"No. I've lost both mother and father in the past few years."

"No husband or prospects?

"No."

"The reason I ask is that I prefer you live in. There is more room in this house than Tabbie and I need. So you would be getting free room and board."

"Would Tabbie accept me?"

"That we would have to see. As well as she accepts anyone, I suppose. It's not easy to say what gets through that shell of hers."

I took a deep breath. "Mr. Casabon, if my references and qualifications are satisfactory, I accept."

He smiled and, once again, I experienced that feeling of a cloud lifting from his features. "Fine. I'm grateful fate sent you my way!"

"God, Mr. Casabon. And...one condition...if anything should ever come up which would make you feel that you have done the wrong thing by hiring me, or if I should decide it's not right, then I go. Is that agreeable?"

But, as men often do, he had ceased to listen to what he felt was a minor point. He was searching through the telephone directory for the number of a doctor he knew.

I didn't repeat my condition, but I took it to heart. If my relationship with my natural mother, whom it was inevitable I would someday meet, would make me wrong for the job, I would have to go. I now knew that someday I would meet my birth mother and the mysterious twin I knew was my half-sister.

Having decided that point, Ron Casabon seemed to put our brief moments of intimacy and sharing behind him, and withdrew into a cool business-like interior. He called the doctor's office and made an appointment for me to go to a clinic and have my foot X-rayed to make certain there were no broken bones. Having done that, he immediately squelched any thoughts I might have had for further conversation by delegating to Ramón, José's older brother, the task of driving me to the clinic and then to the motel to gather my few belongings. To Maria, José and Ramón's mother, he delegated the job of readying a room upstairs for me. Then he retired into his study, nodding briskly with a detached pleasantness that left me feeling isolated. It was Ramón, a handsome, muscular, and sturdy young man, who helped me to the car.

"You are going to stay at Buenaventura, Señorita?"

"I may, Ramón, if it works out. Buenaventura. I like the name."

19

"Yes. It means good luck. You are so much like another señorita—Señorita de la Fuentes who lives next door. You are related?"

"I've never met Señorita Delores. Mr. Casabon said we look alike."

"Yes. *¡Si!* Everything except the eyes. Even then, if yours were not so blue, we would not notice. But you are different. If one talks to you, one knows. You are not like Señorita de la Fuente."

I laughed. "Is that good or bad?"

"I think it is better that you are not like her. There should not be more than one Señorita Loro in the world. She is like a—how do you say? Exploding. Sparks. Fireworks are dangerous but fascinating, no?"

"Do you find Señorita Delores fascinating?"

"Unhappily, yes. But she doesn't give me the time of day."

"Does Señor Casabon find her fascinating?"

"I don't know. Maybe he likes firecrackers. Señora Casabon who died was like that a lot."

In spite of my resolve not to pry into Ron Casabon's business, I felt constrained to ask, "And was Mrs. Casabon a blonde like the lovely Loro?" Then immediately I was ashamed. The words sounded sarcastic, but I really had not meant sarcasm. Or had I? And if so, why? I felt a tinge of flush in my face And reminded myself that my relationship with Ron Casabon was business. Even as I did so, I remembered the firm warmth of Ron Casabon on the horseback ride.

"No, she wasn't. Dark hair. Dark eyes. With a flash in them. Spanish, that one. Like me. She and Mr. Ron quarrel a lot, but I see them quarrel and then make up, too. When she die, people say Mr. Ron killed her. But Mr. Ron didn't. Other people may think so, but we live close to Mr. Ron and we know he didn't do it."

"Oh? People say Mr. Casabon killed her?"

"Mr. Ron did not kill her. If you are going to live in the house, you will see. Mr. Ron is not that kind of man."

"How did she die?"

"On the cliff. She was walking on the cliff and it must have crumbled. Señora Cara was swept down to the rocks below and she died. Some people say she was pushed over. She had been riding with Mr. Ron, and her horse came in alone. Later Mr. Ron came in. They looked for her and found her dead. Mr. Ron say they were riding on the beach and they quarreled, and she rode away mad. He don't see her any more."

"It was at the cliff that I met Mr. Casabon!"

"Yes, I think it was the same place. Mr. Ron was talking about it to me when he came back to get the horse. People talked because Señora Cara's horse came in alone. They say if the cliff crumbled, the horse should have gone over too. She might have gotten off the horse and walked on the cliff. Maybe to see if Mr. Ron was still on the beach. Or maybe she just wanted to walk awhile to –how you say it? Cool off."

"But didn't she know it was dangerous there?"

"Well, yes." He shrugged. "But la Señora don't care. She like danger. She drive cars too fast. She run horses too fast.

Swim too far into the ocean. She liked to worry Mr. Ron. After she died he not the same. Different."

"How different?"

He shrugged. "Crazy things. Walk around all night and not sleep. Sometimes go away for a long time. Stay out at the ranch a lot. Not laugh anymore. But I think Señorita Loro wants to marry him. He's at Casa de la Fuente a lot."

"The next door estate?"

"Yes."

"Do you think they will marry?"

"Why not?" He shrugged again. "Maybe so. Who knows? She's from old family. Much money. Maybe it's a good idea."

So, Señorita Gail, I said to myself, there is Señorita Loro and Señor Ron, who are from local families, and seemingly, on both sides, much money. Then, there is Miss Gail who has not much of anything, and is supposed to help a little girl who very much needs her help. Remember who you are, and what you are here for!

"If things had been fair, it might have been me!" A part of me shouted.

Don't say that, Gail. Do not even think it. It is, by all rights, theirs. Just be happy you have found a good job, a temporary home, and a boss, who, if he is not concerned with your problems, is at least very concerned about his child's problems and is willing to pay you well to help her. Be happy that you had wonderful parents who loved you dearly, made you a part of their good lives, and left you many happy memories. Be happy you have a good education, a good profession, and that God loves you. All of those things are worth a very great deal. Don't you ever forget it. Mr. Ron's and Miss Loro's lives are not your concern.

I deliberately turned my thoughts to Tabbie, who, because of her condition, needed me. We had arrived by then at the doctor's office. I was X-rayed and told I had a bad sprain but no broken bones, and bandaged. The nurse showed me how to wrap the ankle and how to loosen it if there was more swelling. I was given a smile, a prescription, handed a pair of crutches, told to return in two weeks for a checkup, and dismissed.

We went then to the motel where I quickly gathered up my few possessions. Then I hobbled to the office to ask for a refund on the rest of the week's rent I had paid. I did not really expect to get it back. However, after the manager stared for a few minutes through the plate glass at Ramón and the expensive limousine, he handed it over with no comment. Which left me to ponder some unsolvables... such as why an expensive car would do the trick so much more quickly than the plea of a poor but honest face. Then I caught myself shrugging a very Spanish shrug that I hadn't used in Alabama, and wisely let the question lie.

I was still thinking about Tabbie when I asked Ramón to stop at a pet shop.

He gave me a curious glance.

"Well, Tabbie doesn't have a pet, does she?"

"No, Señora Cara did not like pets, except she was fond of horses."

"And Mr. Casabon?"

"I think it's the same for Mr. Ron. He likes horses. He likes the cows and bulls on the ranch. Sometimes he give much money for good bulls, eh? But little pets who live in the house? I don't know. I believe he thinks animals should be useful or you should not own one."

"Well, this pet is for Miss Tabbie, and it will be useful. I hope it will help to bring her out of her shell. Aside from that, usefulness is all very well, but some things maybe should be just for loving, Ramón. You know?"

"Si. Like babies."

"Or little girls. Or kittens. Maybe I'll find a very lovable pet for Miss Tabbie."

"But Miss Tabbie is not going to know about that kind of pet. Miss Tabbie lives somewhere inside her head. She hasn't come out since her mother died. She's in another world."

"There's a poem by Richard Wilbur I learned in college. It goes like this: 'Love calls us to the things of this world.'"

"I think that is a good poem, maybe. You think she will love a puppy or kitten, and the love will make her want to return to this world?"

"Exactly. It says, 'Oh let there be nothing on earth but laundry/ Nothing but rosy hands in the rising steam/ And clean dances done in the sight of heaven.' Anyway it goes on to explain that the soul always wants to be with God, but it has to come back to the complaining body and the imperfect world each day."

"Maybe Tabbie can make it back?"

"Maybe! Or maybe not. But we have to try. You say the problem began when her mother died? That's interesting. Maybe her mother's death was too difficult for her and she couldn't make it back. Anyway, love is going to call her back in the form of, for one thing, a puppy. Now, let's go look for the right one."

By this time he was so interested he accompanied me into the pet shop. We decided the pet would have to be exactly right—not a large, business-like guard dog, nor a pet so small and fragile that it could be easily hurt and thereby heap more guilt and sorrow on poor Tabbie's little shoulders. Therefore, we eliminated the expensive and sensitive thoroughbreds. We finally decided we had found what we wanted in a small pen of mutt types. The one we chose had the general appearance of a dirty dust mop—a coat of black, white, and brown, short legs which carried it in constant investigative circles, an inquisitive nose, a laughing face and busy tongue. It was quick and seemed intelligent enough to get away from an angry or unintentionally cruel child, but affectionate enough also. The clerk assured us that the dog was a good blend of cocker spaniel, poodle, lab and who knows what else, and would be perfect for a little girl. To prove his point he sold us the puppy cheap.

Then we stopped at a bookshop where I purchased some children's books, some sketching pencils and paper, clay, finger paint and watercolors, and we turned back toward Buenaventura.

Maria had put me in the room next to Tabbie's. There was a window that looked out over the sea and one which looked back toward the hills, which turned into mountains to the east; I looked at all that lavish beauty and thanked God that I had landed so well. Or had I? In the back of my mind I was still hearing the solemn rumble and clump of the cave in, and remembering Ron Casabon saying that beauty could be deceptive.

I shivered remembering his words. Below my window there was the green lawn of perhaps one hundred yards, and then that ocean—ever changing, different from what it had been that morning. The sky was now an overcast bronze, colored by the evening sun, tumultuous, heavy, threatening, and that vast and wild, indifferent ocean below was a mirror of burnished, shining gold. Far below me I heard its continuous roar. Muffled by the cliffs, it still sounded like a caged animal. Of course, that was just fancy. It could have been the applause of ten thousand hands, or maybe the sound of the inner workings of the giant machinery of the earth, itself.

I remembered a time when my cousins and I had been playing on the family farm in Alabama, and we had run across an old well which was now only a part of a well—a bent, broken pipe protruding from the ground. The bend had kept it from filling with dirt and leaves. We stooped and put our ears to the pipe and you could hear it—the same sound as that now coming from the ocean.

'Listen," one of my cousins had said, "that's the big engine down in the middle of the earth. It's running the world!"

The day had begun to fade. I opened my suitcase and hung up my clothes. There weren't many of them, but what I had was good. Two suits. Coats, skirts, blouses to go with slacks, which could be interchanged. I had heard of California's interesting climate, which, on the coast was always temperate. So the blouses were for warm days, the coats for cool nights. . There were a few dresses in various stages of formality and informality. One was a dinner dress I had bought it in an optimistic mood one day after watching a slinky model on TV slide into a $60,000 car beside a handsome man in a dinner jacket.

I heard my door open and turned. Tabbie was standing there, staring past me into the room.

"Hello, Tabbie, I'm Gail."

Of course she did not answer, but even so, I believed somewhere in hiding, that little mind of her was picking up signals. She walked past me to the window overlooking the ocean. I stood a moment, with her, and then encircled her with my arm. "Come here, Tabbie, I want to show you something."

I led her to the cage, and pointed out the puppy, which had curled into a small ball on his cushion at the back. Opening the door I drew out the puppy which had awakened and become a frantically joyful bundle of wiggles and wags.

"See the puppy, Tabbie. Isn't he a dear?"

She arched her back and tried to slide off my lap and away from the dog. I locked my arm around her waist to keep her from falling. She began a shrill scream like an animal in pain or the whistle of a steam engine that reverberated around the house, and at the same time began a violent struggle. The puppy, frightened, began struggling to escape from us both. The puppy slipped to the floor, which was okay because of the deep carpet, and then it scooted under the bed. At first, I tried to hold gently to Tabbie, but she also fell on the floor, still screaming and now kicking her heels in the air in a classic tantrum. The scream decibels would have equaled that of a fire engine. I heard footsteps running up the stairs and Ron Casabon flung my door open.

"What in the name of heaven is going on, Miss Templeton?"

"It seems that I have just made the acquaintance of your daughter."

"Well, whatever you have done, don't do it again."

"Don't try to show her a puppy?"

Tabbie's heels were still kicking the air, but she was beginning to quiet. I noted with interest that she was watching her father with one red eye while her little fist dug into the other one. Obviously, she was listening to, and no doubt, understanding the conversation.

"What puppy?"

"The puppy I bought for her this morning at the pet shop."

"Miss Templeton, I do not like dogs in the house, and I did not give you permission to bring a puppy here." Tabbie had now rolled over on her stomach and was looking under the bed for the puppy. I rose and hopped to the door, pushed Ron Casabon through it, and hopped out after him, closing the door behind us.

"Mr. Casabon, you want your daughter to get well, do you not? The puppy is part of her therapy."

"Part of her therapy!"

"Yes. Though Tabbie's screaming startled all of us, I am actually encouraged at her reaction. A part of her problem may be that she is a bit spoiled. She's been allowed to do anything and everything which has crossed her mind. You do not often discipline her, do you?"

"My daughter has been through a lot of trauma, Miss Templeton."

"Just as I thought. Let me work with her, Mr. Casabon. It will be painful for all three of us in the beginning, but I believe I can help her. Will you wait just a moment? I have my résumé and some letters of reference in my suitcase, and I'll get them for you. You will find that I have had special training for dealing with disturbed children. I expect to be able to use that training to help Tabbie."

I slipped quickly back in my room. There was no sign of the puppy, but Tabbie's legs were sticking out from under the bed, where the two of them seem to be getting along very well. I retrieved my papers from my briefcase and hurried back to give them to Ron Casabon. He glanced at them and then began again.

"Miss Templeton, I will not allow my child to be experimented with and I'll probably arrive promptly should she do that sort of screaming again. Good Lord, Miss Templeton, can you expect me not to react?"

"No. It's perfectly normal and good for a father to be concerned about his child. But if she is to be in my care, Mr.

Casabon, it will require a certain amount of trust between us. After you go through those papers, I should not be too much of a stranger any longer. I should be recognized as professionally capable of handling an autistic child. If you find splinters under her nails, or bruises on her neck, interfere. Otherwise, let me do my job."

His eyes narrowed. "And you propose to do your job by making Tabbie scream?"

"Has she ever screamed before?"

"Well, yes," he admitted reluctantly.

"When?"

"I do not make notations of such things."

"Let me guess. It's when she wants something different from what those around expect of her. Were you mistreating her at those times?"

"Certainly not. But I am her father, I..."

"Mr. Casabon, somewhere inside that shell of Tabbie's there is a frightened child who has withdrawn from the world. We have to call her back to this world and insist that she come. She does not want to. She wants to stay in a dark, warm place she considers safe. If I take Tabbie in my arms for a hug, she may scream. If I try to comb her hair, she may scream. If I make her put on her shoes she may scream because I am threatening her protective fantasy world and dragging her back to a world which has become too big and too frightening for a four year old to deal with. But I must be allowed to interact with Tabbie according to my training and instincts as a teacher, as a woman, and, well..."

"Yes?"

"As someone who loves her."

For a moment his eyes softened and fell, but when he raised them they were flashing dark fire again. "I will be the final authority for Tabbie, Miss Templeton. I will give you freedom within bounds, but in the end I know and will do what is best for her."

"I hope so, Mr. Casabon."

He turned to go, but, as he did so, a girl appeared behind him at the top of the stairs. At first she was looking at him, and then beyond him at me. As she stared, I saw shock cross her features. And it must have crossed mine, also, because it was as though I was looking in a mirror.

CHAPTER III

"Loro, meet what is evidently a long lost twin of yours, Miss Gail Templeton."

She did not step forward to meet me, but slowly made her way to stand by Ron, continuing to stare without speaking. We were the same size, and not too different in age. Her hair was golden with curl in it. Mine was straight, light, naturally streaked blonde. Her eyes were a cool hazel, which, I later learned, changed color with her moods and the colors she wore. There was a bold directness in her look, an arch to her well-defined nostrils, which let one know she was accustomed to getting her way. But if all that failed to convince, her immaculate grooming and very expensive dress would have. She wore one of those deceptively simple things, white, with a cascade of embroidered flowers spilling to the hem. I thought ruefully of my new wardrobe of which I had been so proud, and knew that the price of that dress would buy two just like it. I saw an imperious lift of her chin as she turned from me to Ron.

"Who is that?"

"You weren't listening, Loro. I just introduced you to Miss Templeton."

"And who is Miss Templeton? What is she doing here?"

"Miss Templeton is to be Tabby's teacher."

"And where did she come from?"

"I had the good fortune to find Miss Templeton on the beach this morning. Actually I thought she was you."

"Found her on the beach and moved her into your house to be your child's teacher?"

"It happens that Miss Templeton is that private teacher for Tabbie for whom I have been searching. I was just going over her qualifications with her." He indicated the papers in his hand. "She has a Master's Degree and some top references from some important people in her field.

"But, whoa! I had almost forgotten. I was invited to dinner, wasn't I?" He took her arm to turn her, but she pulled back.

"Does she also talk?"

"Talks, sings, quotes poetry. Whatever you would like," I said.

"Where did you come from? You aren't from here."

"No, I'm from the South."

"Los Angeles?"

I had to smile. Even being in California so short a time I had already encountered the native Californian's propensity for thinking that his state is the whole nation, and nothing much exists east of the Sierras. "Alabama."

At this, she turned and looked at Ron. He, also, smiled. "Yes, Loro, there is an Alabama. A southern state located between Georgia on the east and Mississippi on the west."

And is noted for its shipbuilding, exporting of pine timber and cotton...and, unfortunately, importing fire ants and cogon grass, I wanted to add, but listened to my better judgment and said nothing. Which was just as well because the imperious Miss de la Fuente suddenly decided to dismiss my existence completely. "Yes, we'll be late," she said, and walked away, down the hall toward the stairs.

Ron Casabon looked at me briefly then turned and followed her. I couldn't read his expression, and after he left I hoped that mine had not too blatantly betrayed the gamut of emotions I had experienced—shock, dismay, and the residue of anger from my discussion about Tabbie with her father.

I limped back into my room and found Tabbie standing just inside the door. She immediately dodged around it and down the hall, out of sight. I strolled over to the window and stood looking out over the ocean, feeling rather dreadfully alone—more alone than I had ever felt before in my life. In the distance, the red sky dipped down into the beautiful turbulent water. I wondered why I felt depressed. It was only my third day in California, and already God had given me so much—but, as is often the case, what I had gained only served to underline what I did not have. Was life always going to be like this? Climbing one mountain only to find a higher range ahead? Does where you are never matter as much as where you are not?

I did not realize that I was weeping until I reached up to brush the tears from my face. I felt an unbearable sense of loss. My Alabama home had been taken from me. My claim to a family had somehow slipped when I found out that I had been adopted. My adoptive father had died, and then my mother. Had I ever been an intrinsic part of that family? I had come to California seeking a home. I knew that then, although I had been kidding myself that it was only curiosity. And instead of a home I had found an arrogant and difficult employer, whom I was horrified to find myself attracted to, a little girl who had already rejected my affection, a beautiful and luxurious home in which I was a stranger, a whole ethnic background to which also I was a stranger, and a younger sister who looked down her nose at me and addressed me as "her" in my presence.

The room had darkened. The light from the setting sun and the ocean gave it a faint rose-colored glow. I straightened my shoulders, looked out on that vast expanse and prayed. Then I leaned back and talked to myself. "Oh, me of little faith," I said, misquoting the Bible. "When did anything in this old and cold world ever get done without a mountain of trouble? What was that saying my dad used to quote? 'It takes a lot of manure to make the roses grow!' And God turns evil-smelling manure or dead fish into gorgeous roses with the most beautiful, delicate scent and petals like the most expensive satin. We can't dissolve into tears and fears. Sit up straight and look the devil in the eye. You're a fighter, Gail!"

I got up, hobbled to the bathroom where I washed my face and looked at myself in the mirror. "So someone scored a knockout on you in the first few minutes of the first round," I told myself. "You can handle that. It shouldn't shock you that you're younger sister immediately hated you. From what I have heard and seen Loro would think the world too crowded with two Loros in it. Women don't even like for other women to wear the same dress, much less the same face." I combed my hair and smiled at my private joke. I had everything under control again, and was glad I did because there was a knock on the door. It opened and Maria came in bearing a tray.

"You forget to eat, I think," she said, "But it's best to eat up here with your bad foot. Mr. Ron went out. Do you like Mexican food?"

"I think I'm going to like it very much. It smells delicious."

"I think you will like it. Tonight we are having *chili rellenos*—green chilies stuffed with cheese—and chicken enchiladas. I brought bread and tortillas both, so you can choose the one you like"

"Do you serve Mexican food when Mr. Ron is home?" I asked after she had showed me how to butter, salt and roll the tortilla and seemed determined to stay and see that I did the Mexican meal justice.

"Mr. Ron comes from a Latino family. His grandfather was Mestizo—Mexican Indian. Like most of us, his family is mixed with Spanish. When the Spaniards first came to California, some of them owned a lot of land, and some of those were Mr. Ron's ancestors. The family lost the land and lost their money when some of them drink too much. Mr. Ron has always said he would get his share back again. He is a good lawyer. Makes lots of money. I think he has gotten much of his family's money back. He's even gotten the old family ranch back. It's up in the mountains to the east."

"Mr. Ron's wife, Cara, she was also Mexican." I remarked.

"Oh yes. Si. I think Mr. Ron wants always to have a wife who is Mexican like him." I felt a little pang. So much for me. As far as he was concerned, I'm northern-European, English-Irish, like my parents were!

"What was she like...Cara?" I knew I shouldn't ask, but did so anyway.

"Oh very pretty. I think beautiful. Black hair. Black eyes. Skin like rich cream. And full of life."

"Were they happy together?"

"Well, sometimes. Up times. Down times. You know what I mean?"

"No." I played dumb in order to get more information.

"Sometimes they, like kids say, 'high'. She high on cocaine, he high with love for her. Full of life. Other times quarreling. She's saying cross and ugly things, and he's moody and angry. He leaves. Goes to ranch, stays two, three days. Or stays and sleeps at office in Santa Barbara. She looks around for something else. Goes out at night alone. I think he is not too happy. Some people say he got mad and kill her, but I don't think he'd do that."

"I see." The picture she was painting was unsettling and even frightening. But I had finished my meal, and Maria began to gather the tray and dishes.

"You like Mexican?"

"Love it. Maria you are a good cook." I said, making a mental note to go easy on the beans and tortillas or my size six would not be that long. The puppy, which had escaped under the bed during the bout with Tabbie and her father, came wagging out at the smell of food, puddling the floor and smiling happily as it demolished a small piece of enchilada I had saved for it. Maria volunteered to return the puppy to the cage and mop up the puddle, and I thanked her.

"Mr. Ron doesn't care if you have the dog?"

"I don't think he likes the dog's being here. But he was too upset about Tabbie's screaming to say too much. The dog is a part of Tabbie's therapy. I believe the puppy will be very good for her. There is something magical which goes on between children and animals."

"I hope he lets her have it. That little girl needs something like a puppy she can cuddle and feel safe with.

"By the way, where is Tabbie?"

"Playing in the sunroom, I think. Ramón is watching her. Don't worry. I will put her to bed."

"This time."

"Well, only until you can manage with your bad foot. She's not always easy to handle. Sometimes she fights, and I have to get one of the boys to help."

"Thank the Lord for you and your boys, Maria. When I start trying to get through to her I may have to call for some help from time to time."

Maria took the tray and departed. I hobbled into pajamas and got into bed. In the middle of the night, I awoke to the sound of the puppy whining and clawing at his cage, and, beyond that, I heard the sound of the ocean. The wind had come up and the surf had increased its roar. The big house seemed threatening and dark.

I got out of bed and went to the window to look out toward the ocean. There was a full moon, making a silvery path across the water and it was eerily beautiful. A boat bobbed in the water behind the Fuente estate. I started to turn back toward my bed when I saw a shadow separate itself from the shrubbery near the stairs down the cliffs and walk across the yard. I stepped out of sight behind my curtain and continued to watch. The shadow was a man. Ron Casabon? I didn't think so. He stopped a moment below my window and stared up at it and toward the window next to it—Tabbie's. In a moment, he turned and walked toward the street at the front of the house.

Just then I became conscious that the puppy's whines had become loud and mournful yaps. I unlocked the cage and took it into my bed, knowing that it was a bad thing to do, and that never again would it sleep contentedly in its own bed at night. But that shadow had made me uneasy, and the pup's friendly warmth and wiggle brought me comfort. It snuggled immediately to my side and gave a contented sigh. The surf didn't sound so angry then, and the dark fears moved a little further away. I fell into a deep sleep and didn't wake again until daylight.

As soon as I was up and dressed, I hobbled to the adjoining room to catch a glimpse of my pupil before she was awake. She lay on her side in a nightgown embroidered with dainty yellow roses. Her little face was relaxed, caught up in the intense business of sleep. I put my hand on her little head and prayed for her. Then, because I knew somehow, even in sleep, her little spirit was listening, I spoke to her aloud.

"Tabbie, dear, I am your new teacher. My name is Gail. We are going to have a lot of fun together and learn many new things." I sat down on the bed beside her and caressed her dark curls. "Dearest little girl, I love you and God loves you. Come back to us, Tabbie." I stroked her cheek.

The large dark eyes flew open. She backed away, and for the first time stared me full in the face. I smiled at her. She sat up, locked her hands around her knees and rocked back and forth, waiting for full wakefulness to come. Then she bounded from the bed and flew to our connecting door, opened it and disappeared inside. When I got to the door she was kneeling at the puppy's cage, poking in one inquisitive finger, which the puppy was licking with relish.

"Tabbie, the puppy's name is Andrew. We're going to call him Andy."

I had opened my door to the hall so that I would hear the downstairs sounds of breakfast in time to limp to the dining room and save Maria the trip upstairs with a tray.

"They seem to be getting on very well, Miss Templeton." Ron Casabon was standing in the doorway.

"Yes. Does that mean we have your permission to keep him?"

"Oh? My permission is required?" He lifted an eyebrow.

So, we're back to that, I thought. "It would be nice to have it," I said.

"I still question the need of a dog."

"Scripture says that God blesses those who are kind to his little animals."

"Ah. And where does it say that?"

"I believe you'll find it somewhere in the book of Ecclesiastes. Or maybe Song of Solomon."

"You read the Bible, Miss Templeton?"

"Yes. It's a very good book. A best seller."

"Are you one of those good born-again Christians, Miss Templeton?"

"All good Christians are born again, Mr. Casabon. It is a stipulation established by the Founder."

"Is that also in the Song of Solomon? I understand that is an X-rated book."

"No, it's in the New Testament. Song of Solomon is X-rated depending on how you think of such things. Is sex dirty, Mr. Casabon, or is it an expression of true love, which is beautiful?" I bit my tongue. Why had I said that?

"Ah..." He stared at me soberly. "Is your dog going to puddle my carpets, Miss Templeton?"

"He may. But what is a small puddle compared to a little girl's happiness?" I gestured to the dog and child. She had found the key on my dresser, unlocked the cage, taken the puppy out, and was clutching it in her lap as she sat on the floor. The face of both child and dog expressed profound happiness. "We will clean up the puddles and do our best to see he is housebroken as soon as possible."

"Dogs, particularly small dogs, have bad habits. They puddle the floor, and these are expensive floors. They yap at night. They tear up shoes and books. I really dislike lap dogs, and anything that is altogether useless."

"Look at them Mr. Casabon. Do you really think that dog is useless? Some things are made just to be loved, Mr. Casabon—flowers, sunsets, little girls, little dogs. I think they have their places in the order of things. The floors may be expensive, but they are a long way from being worth as much as your daughter is.

"The floors are permanent. My daughter's condition is hopeless. Still, we must live, somehow circling around her as you would circle around a wreck on the highway. She may have fleeting observations or an affection for the puppy, but it probably would not be worth a stain on the floor, or survive as long."

"My how pessimistic you are, Mr. Casabon. Who told you your daughter's condition is hopeless? Hopeless is a big word."

"The doctors."

"Pfft. What do they know? Some of them are pretty dense, particularly when it comes to knowing about the human spirit."

"You are an authority on the human spirit?"

"Why not? As much as they are, surely. I'm at least learning to love Tabbie, and I don't know if they do or not.

Right now she is not able to stand up for or plead for her own rights, and I believe she has rights. I believe every child has rights and to accept my gift of a puppy is one of her rights. So I'll do her pleading for her."

"Tabbie cannot care for a dog. You're wasting your efforts if you think she'll eventually be normal."

"Normal or not, she'll love the puppy. I believe she already does. And until or even if she is never able, I'll care for the dog."

"And I'll not have you cluttering up the place and inconveniencing my guests and the servants with a parade of experiments on Tabbie."

"Inconveniencing, Mr. Casabon? Why don't you simply put Tabbie in a dark room and lock the door? Occasionally hand food in to her? Then you and your guests would not suffer inconvenience."

He looked at me a long moment with those hard, marble-like incredibly dark eyes. "The dog can stay, Miss Templeton. But get permission from me before you try any more experiments with Tabbie."

"Why yes, Mr. Casabon. We're going to try an experiment this afternoon—with finger-paint. Would you like to give us permission now, or would you rather come in and do some finger-painting yourself? In addition, as soon as I can walk again, we will go down to the beach and look for some anemones and abalones to play with and enjoy. Then she'll find out what a big and interesting world she lives in. I will get permission from you for any thing of a controversial nature, but for normal procedures in the teacher-student relationship, I intend to take responsibility myself. If that is not satisfactory to you, I don't believe I can stay in this job."

During my tirade, his eyes had gone from disdain, to angry cold black, to a softening, "When can we go to the beach to search for anemones? I'm no good at finger painting."

Caught off guard I began to stammer. "Why, I...I don't know. When is my ankle going to be healed?"

He turned and started down the stairs. "Let's ride horses down tomorrow after breakfast."

I didn't know whether to laugh or throw my crutches after him. I limped slowly back to my room. Tabbie was still hugging and caressing Andy. My heart gave a lurch as I saw her handle the puppy carefully. Autistic children usually do not show that much care. I had been worried that Tabbie might hurt the pet, but she encircled the puppy in a gentle hug and bent to hide her face in the ragged, tousled coat. The tension caused by my argument with Ron Casabon began to ease away, and I felt myself smiling. When the child stood up and both girl and puppy ran from the room, I did not object. I didn't think it would be too difficult to find either of them later. Wherever they would be, they would be together.

I have my prayer time in the morning. By the time I had prayed, made my bed, tidied the room, freshened my lipstick and hobbled downstairs Ron Casabon had eaten and gone. Perhaps I had hoped he would be. And then, perhaps not. Was that a tinge of disappointment I felt, or had I deliberately dawdled? At any rate, I was relieved that I could eat in peace.

In the dining room an urn of coffee and breakfast rolls stood on the sideboard. The rolls—*pan dulces*, I soon learned to call them—were homemade by Maria and her daughter Sequestra, a shy girl of fifteen who kept out of sight in the kitchen. I would usually catch only brief glimpses of her, dusting living room furniture or running a sponge around shining fixtures in one of the bathrooms.

"Sit down, Miss Templeton. I bring eggs," Maria called from the kitchen.

"Not too many, please, and call me Gail."

"Gail is pretty name. You're like a wind-gale, no? I hear you tell Mr. Ron that Tabbie gotta have dog. I say good for Miss Gail! That little girl needs someone. Mr. Ron he loves her, but not understand little girls."

"Yes, and I guess this 'gale' had better quiet down or I'll be looking for a new job."

"No, I don't think so. Mr. Ron have his head in the air too long. Doesn't see too much. Doesn't want to see, you know? Like he's…what you call it? Ice. Ice inside. You got a warm heart. You good for him."

"Good for him?" I asked, puzzled.

"Mr. Ron is Mexican, like me. Mexican are fire or ice. Ice is no good for Mr. Ron. You like *huevos rancheros*?"

"*Huevos…?* What are they?"

"Eggs cooked Mexican. Fried or scrambled?"

"Scrambled. I can't stand watery yellow eyes looking at me in the morning."

"I understand." She went back to the kitchen to prepare the eggs while I munched on a pan dulce. It was delicious.

The coffee was hot and served with real cream. I was sipping it when Maria came back with the huevos rancheros and refried beans. The hot sauce on the eggs quickly brought tears to my eyes, which I tried to cover by taking a quick gulp of coffee. It did nothing to cool me off.

"Where is Tabbie?" I asked.

"She is playing in the back patio. The little dog is with her. I sent Sequestra to watch her."

"I was a bit afraid of Tabbie's hurting the dog unintentionally."

"I don't think she'd do that. Tabbie has never been mean. She got strange when her mother died and when people who talk too much said Mr. Ron made her die. Which is wrong, of course."

"But I've heard they quarreled a lot. Anger and desperation can sometimes make people do bad things."

"Trouble, yes. Trouble between them. But Mr. Ron does not do such things. I know him for a long time."

Maria was becoming indignant, so I let it go. She returned to the kitchen, and I cleaned up the eggs, carefully evading, as much as possible, the hot sauce. As I sipped the coffee, I could not help replaying in my mind again and again the scene with Ron that morning. His anger softening, his eyes becoming tender as I talked about my love for his daughter, and then becoming playful as he said he would accompany us to the beach. I wondered if he really would go anemone hunting with us the next day.

CHAPTER IV

It was one of those sparkling, clear California days full of sunlight, blue skies and the promise of good things. I opened my eyes to see Tabbie at the edge of my bed watching me sleep, puppy on one arm and the other thumb stuck in her mouth. I smiled and stretched. This had to be a good day. I had survived my first set-to with Ron Casabon and I was going horseback riding with him on the beach!—provided, of course, that he remembered it.

Should I feel this secret delight? Ron Casabon was a pagan. Handsome, charming pagans are not good things for their daughter's teachers to dwell upon.

The puppy was licking Tabbie's ear, and she was laughing and trying to twist away from it. I noticed that Tabbie had evidently entered my room by the hall door and left it open. Though Ron's room was on the ground floor, fearful that he would be attracted by his daughter's high-pitched giggles and happen by again while I was still in my nightgown, I rose and shut the door.

In spite of my good intentions, and the stern lectures I was giving myself, I was a bit disappointed not to find him at the breakfast table, but Tabbie and I had breakfast together. Which was a first for us, a sign that she was beginning to accept me into her life. After breakfast, we went to the back lawn to play ball with the puppy. Girl and dog were running wildly and tumbling over each other when Ramón appeared.

"Señor Casabon is waiting at the barn for two señoritas, Señorita Templeton and Señorita Tabbie, if you are ready to go riding."

"Oh yes! Tabbie, let's go see your daddy and ride the horses."

At that, the child hesitated and began to look frightened, but Ramón took her in his arms and began to speak soothingly in Spanish, and with the puppy following, we made our way to the barn where Ron and Ramón's brother José were waiting with the horses.

"Ah, you are prompt, Miss Templeton. I appreciate that."

I handed my crutches to José and mounted a pretty palomino mare. Ramón handed Tabbie up to Ron, but she immediately started screaming and kicking. Ron wrestled with her briefly, muttering in Spanish, and then handed her back to Ramón with a curse.

"Bring her to me," I called. "And bring the puppy."

Ramón handed her up to me. At first, she screamed and struggled, but I cuddled and soothed her, and she grew quieter. After Ramón handed up the puppy she settled quietly on the saddle in front of me, holding the puppy and sucking her thumb.

"You see our Miss Templeton is a miracle worker, Ramón. Tabbie thinks highly of her already." Ron said, and I caught a hint of sarcasm in his voice as he turned his horse to lead us down the trail.

Oh Lord! I thought, and I really was talking to Him. I'm doomed if I don't help Tabbie, and doomed if I do.

If the esteemed Ron Casabon was peeved, I decided, that was his problem and not mine. He could deal with it. I refused to be disheartened on such a beautiful day.

By now we were under the cliffs, down along the shore. It was so lovely, achingly beautiful—the wild, sparkling water, topped by white caps, bright sun, and sand. I was falling in love with it all! My heart ached at the thought that someday I would have to leave it, but I would not think about that on this day.

The horse must have caught my joy, because it began a gentle rocking gallop along the sand. Tabbie squealed, this time with laughter, clutching the puppy close in her arms, and Ron followed on his buckskin. About a mile from the spot where we had come down the cliffs, I found a little sheltered cove, away from the wind, with bright sand, colored pebbles, and a few large rocks.

"This is a good place to look for anemones," Ron said. I was glad to hear it. I really knew nothing about anemones, having only read about them in my books about California. We got down from our horses. Ron weighed down the reins with two of the larger rocks. I asked him to come near so I could hold his shoulder as I hopped to a boulder to sit down, but he picked me up easily and deposited me on a rock where I could look into the clear water. "You see, here's one already," he said, showing us a flower-like creature with would-be petals waving gently with the motion of the water.

"Can we touch it?" I asked

"Try it and see." His tone was teasing. I bravely stuck my finger in the center of the flower and the tiny tentacles closed around it like a baby's fist.

"Tabbie, you have to try this," I said, guiding her little finger to the anemone that closed around it. She squealed with delight, and dropped the puppy in the water. It splashed a moment, found its legs, climbed out, and shook itself indignantly, wetting all of us in the process. Tabbie, meanwhile, began to run, still squealing and laughing, from one tidal pool to another, finding anemones and putting her little fingers in their tentacles.

I hopped down from the rock, and taking her hand limped to where the waves were washing up on the beach. She dashed backward and forward, following the water as it washed to the shore and retreated to the ocean. One powerful wave washed further ashore than the others did. She screamed and ran to me, knocking me off balance, and both of us went down in the water. I caught her in my arms, rolled over on the sand and began to show her the shells at the waterline. But she was still in a gale of giggles and she deliberately splashed water on me. I retaliated by splashing water back on her.

"Hey, you are getting all wet, and you are going to be most uncomfortable riding back to the house." Ron said. He stooped to pick Tabbie up, but she dodged away from him and ran toward the waves, where she picked up water and splashed it all over his spotless, well-pressed khakis. "So that's the way it is!" Ron yelled, and went after her, polished boots and all, up and down the beach, in and out of the water, man, child and puppy. There issued a brief and lively water fight, from which they both emerged thoroughly wet and laughing. Then she ran toward him and pushed him, and he pretended to be knocked down beside me, half in the water. Whereupon she dug fistfuls of sand put it on his back.

"Tabbie, Tabbie, that's enough," I said, "let's not bury Daddy." I pulled her down in my lap and hugged her. The puppy came over and plopped down nearby. Abruptly she lay back in my arms and stuck her thumb in her mouth. Ron lay back in the sand, studying the sky for a moment and then turned to face me.

"Miss Templeton..."

"Yes?"

"Don't you think at this point 'Miss Templeton' and 'Mr. Casabon' are out of place?"

"Yes indeed. You could call me Gail."

"Gail, yes. That sounds better. And you could call me Ron."

"May I ask why a Hispanic mother would name her son Ronald?"

He laughed. "Try Ronaldo. Ronaldo Alexandro Casabon."

"Ah, that's better. It suits you."

"And Gail suits you."

He lay back on the sand, and, still clutching Tabby, I scooted to a rock and rested my back against it. It was so peaceful—the sound of the waves, the cry of the gulls. He lay for a long time on his back, his arms shielding his eyes from the sun. Then he rose and looked at Tabbie.

"Asleep," I said.

"Worn out," Ron said. "She's never had this much activity before."

"Yes. It's all rather wonderful."

"Wonderful?"

"The water, the sleeping child, the sunshine. Oh, everything!"

He looked at me frowning, and then looked away. "Yes, one forgets."

"Forgets?"

"The ocean, the sky, the sunlight, the child. One forgets."

"How could one forget?"

He traced a line in the sand. "One gets sidetracked. All of my life I have been wanting, wanting, wanting. I work hard to get them—things." I heard a trace of accent as he let his guard down. "Now Cara is gone. Tabbie is—as she is. Some people think I killed my wife. You have heard that?"

"I've heard some things. Yes."

"I'm wondering if the work and worry was worth it."

"I did not know Cara. Tabbie is worth it."

He looked at the sleeping child and smiled. "You may be right... Well, Miss Templeton—Gail—let's get on the horses, wet clothing and all. It is time to go home. You carry the little dog and I'll carry my daughter, if you can hand her up to me." He retrieved the reins of the two horses and brought them over, mounted his, and I handed the child up to him, and, balancing the puppy, got on my palomino.

We were half way home when we saw a figure on horseback riding toward us. It was Loro, and she scrutinized us closely as we approached. "Well, I see you have had an outing—swim party—clothes and all."

"Yes. We had a hunting expedition with Tabbie. We were hunting anemones, and it involved getting wet," Ron said.

"Very educational, I am sure."

"Most educational."

"My mother would like to speak to Miss Templeton," she said. "As soon as possible. And you, too, Ron, if you can come over. Maybe this afternoon?"

I gave a start and my heart began to pound. Oh no! Here it is!

"Why, that is no problem, Loro. We will change our wet clothing and be over soon afterwards."

"I believe Mama would like to see you separately."

He looked at me swiftly, seeing something in my face. "Why separately?"

"I've never met Señora Fuente. I'm sure I do not know."

"What is it, Loro, that your mother wants to speak to Miss Templeton about?"

"How should I know? I just obey Mother's commands. Maybe the decorations for fiesta? Or something else so earth-shattering?"

He looked at me again. "I see. Okay. We'll get Tabbie down, change, and be over shortly. Tell your mother."

I left a sleeping Tabbie in Marie's care, took a quick shower changed clothes, and was back downstairs to meet Ron—who had quickly showered and changed also-- within thirty minutes. He sensed my apprehension, and said nothing. We walked silently, me hobbling on my crutches, Ron occasionally touching my arm when we came to rough places.

Whereas Buenaventura held to a Southwestern theme— it was fresh and modern. Casa de la Fuente, on the other hand, was redolent with age and tradition. The floors were polished marble, the walls a chalk white, the furniture heavy, carved and dark, alternating with ironwork. There were various distinguished ancestral portraits lining the curving staircase. However, looking closely I could see small signs of lack of care, and too much age. The rugs were lovely, but worn around the edges. There were almost invisible webs of dust in the corners.

The Señora was waiting with Loro in the hall. As I approached her, my footsteps, already slow because of the crutches, became slower. A couple of times I hesitated and stopped and Ron looked at me curiously.

She was a very distinguished woman, immaculate from her sleek hairdo, the immaculate pale pink silk suit, to the pointed slippers. She was still quite beautiful, though she had to be in her late forties. At first glance, one would think she was a cold woman, but one look in her bright blue eyes dispelled that idea. As we walked toward her she was watching me closely, taking in every inch from my sandals and crutches, to my red flowered skirt, my red sweater top, and then up to my face and hair. She said nothing, but continued to stare in my face.

"Señora?" Ron said.

"Yes, yes, Ron...I, I...pardon. I must sit down." She went to a white leather sofa and sat down, gesturing to other chairs as she did so. Lora sat in a nearby chair and I sat gingerly on the edge of a loveseat, but Ron went to her and stopped beside her.

"You are all right, Señora?"

"No Ron, I'm a foolish old woman." Unexpectedly she reached out to hug his shoulder and he embraced her and patting her back as he did so. In a moment, she sat back and wiped her eyes with a lace-edged handkerchief, and Ron came and sat down by me.

So this is the young lady my Loro has told me about! Your resemblance to my daughter is astonishing! I was really taken aback for a moment."

"I was rather astonished myself," I murmured.

"How did you come to be Tabbie's teacher?"

"We met on the beach. Ron mistook me for Loro." I nodded at my half-sister. "We started talking."

"And then you sprained your ankle?"

"I know it sounds odd, but that is really what happened."

"It really is odd," she said slowly, again questioning me with her eyes.

"Please, Señora," Ron said. "I believe you are frightening my daughter's teacher. She really is a teacher of exceptional children. I have had her checked out. She is from a fine old family in Alabama, and her credentials are impeccable. If you frighten her away I will lose a good teacher for whom I have been searching for a long time."

Again, the Señora looked me over carefully, taking her time. And, again, I looked her over, my heart pounding. This was the mother who had given me away so long ago. We were the same height, had the same blonde complexion, and my eyes were the same light turquoise as were hers. She had a middle-age plumpness, but it was not unpleasing.

"You are from Alabama," she said.

"Yes."

"Recently?"

"Only a few days ago."

"Alabama is a long way. Why are you here?"

"Gail had finished college, worked a bit, and then decided to see a bit of the world, Señora." Ron. said. "And I thank heaven she did."

"So you are a college graduate?"

"Graduated with honors," Ron intervened again.

"Oh my. So intelligent."

"Please, Señora, you flatter me."

At that moment, a man entered the room. He was a little shorter than Ron, but would still be classified as tall because of an extreme slimness. He was dark, obviously Hispanic, which Loro and the señora were not, well built, and smiling as he extended a hand.

"Ron! Good to see you again."

"Luis." Ron said, with considerably less enthusiasm, and slowly extended a hand for shaking.

Señora Fuente seemed to come to herself. "Luis, this is our new neighbor, Miss Templeton. My stepson, Luis."

He hurried to me, took my hand, and bent over it in the old world way. "So this is the beautiful señorita I have heard about. Welcome to Casa de la Fuente, Señorita."

"Thank you," I extricated my hand.

"Yes indeed, *Mamacita,* she does indeed look like our Loro. Could we have long lost cousins in—where did you say you are from, Señorita?"

"Alabama."

"I see. Well, are you Hispanic?"

"No. I..no…"

"Hablas Espanol?" Señora asked. And suddenly I was very much aware that she had used the familiar form of the verb such as is used only to close friends and members of the family. In that moment I knew that my birth Mother had accepted me. I smiled at her, and in that smile she knew that, for better or worse, I had accepted her.

"No, Señora. I do not speak Spanish. Perhaps I can learn."

"And it will be my pleasure to teach you." Luis said quickly.

"Well, I..."

"Miss Templeton's time is pretty restricted." Ron said gruffly.

"Ah, come now, Ron. You are not such a slave driver? Miss Templeton and I will find some time together for the lessons. Isn't this possible, Miss Templeton?"

"I would love to learn Spanish. But Tabbie and I are just learning to work together. Perhaps a little later, Luis."

"But I was forgetting why I asked you to come over," the Señora said. "Ron, Cinco de Mayo is almost upon us. Fiesta days, Gail. The Fuentes will be giving our annual spring celebration. You must both come. Ron, I know you dress caballero. And Gail..."

"Yes?"

"You will wear the fiesta dress."

"Thank you for the invitation. But I..."

"It is not just an invitation. It is a command. She does not know about Mexican mamas." My heart jumped, and I gulped, but she was looking innocently at Ron. "Does she, *Hijo*? You see, Ron's parents are dead, also, and I have been his mama ever since he moved next door. No, you see, Mexican mamas are very bossy."

"I see." I did, and my heart melted with joy. My natural mother was giving me an invitation to be her daughter. But why had she not asked the obvious question—Are you my daughter? Because, in my heart, I had recognized my birth mother and was confident that she recognized me as her daughter. But why didn't she speak out? Why did I feel that she wanted me, also, to keep quiet? Of course! Because her husband and children had never been told!"

"If Ron is willing."

"Ron is willing," Ron said with one of his rare smiles. "Will you accompany me, Señorita Gail?"

Loro, who had been unusually quiet, was quick to interject, "No! Gail can go with Luis. Ron is my date. He promised me last year he would be my date this year."

"And I shall be more than happy to accompany Miss Gail," Luis said.

"Well, it seems as though you have things settled," I said, with a smile at Loro, who quickly looked aside. "Thank you Señor Luis. I will be happy to be your date."

"And I shall look forward to seeing you here," Señora said, and dismissed us with a nod. Linking her hand in Luis' arm, she left the room, and Loro showed us to the door.

We walked slowly back to the house. As we left, my emotions, which I had managed to hold to, just barely, began to rise to the surface and tears began to roll down my cheeks. When we got back to Buenaventura Ron steered me toward the patio, and sat me down in a chair there, sitting down beside me. He fished in his pocket for a handkerchief and handed it to me.

"And now you will perhaps tell me what that was about," he said.

I wiped my eyes. "I can't."

"Try." he said.

I waited a few minutes lost in many thoughts. When I was in control again, I said, "I can't right now."

"Why not?"

"Because I will be weeping all afternoon. It's a long story, and I have Tabbie to check on. You have a right to know, and I will tell you, but give me a few days to digest it. It's all so overwhelming."

With a Hispanic man's innate graciousness he agreed, and did not ask me again. Days passed and my ankle healed. I was able to ramble around, getting acquainted with the horses, the barn, and Maria's husband (who worked in town), and the men who worked on the ranch and occasionally came in on business. It was a beautiful estate, and Tabbie and I spent wonderful moments wandering among and examining flowers and shrubs. Once or twice I looked up at the windows of the Fuente estate and caught a glimpse of a figure disappearing behind a drape. Was it my mother, or Loro, or that interesting character, Luis, Loro's half-brother?

And I would spend hours gazing at the Pacific, wondering at that impossible expanse, thinking of God and talking to Him.

Ron joined Tabbie and me often on horseback trips to the beach. Each time the magic was the same. The ocean was healing all three of us—Tabbie, Ron, and me, as we played in the sand and water. All three of us began to wear our cut-off jeans and come back home sandy, wet and relaxed. When Tabbie would throw water on me, I would catch her and pretend to be a big bear, eating her, or roll with her in the sand and water, to the accompaniment of her wild squeals and giggles. And then I would look up to see Ron looking at us with a wistful expression, until Tabbie began to become bolder and tease him and he would catch her and nuzzle her neck, asking for kisses, until she would give in and give him a hug and kiss.

And each time we would all three draw a little closer. I would wonder…where is it going, Lord? What are you doing here? Ron was always a perfect gentleman, and I tried hard to keep my mind and thoughts where they should be. But I was also a little frightened. I knew deep in my heart that this was a man who got what he wanted, and more and more I was convinced that he wanted me. That he would weave a web around me until, one way or another, he would have me. The thought was disconcerting, and I decided firmly that would not be. I could not marry him. I am a Christian, I told myself. I could not marry this beguiling pagan, and anything else was unthinkable.

One time when I had been walking along the cliffs alone I returned to the house to find Luis standing in the back patio smoking a cigarette.

"Ah, Señorita Gail, are you ready for a Spanish lesson?"

"As soon as I find appropriate time, Mr. Fuente," I responded. I sat down and gestured for him to do the same.

"You are working much with little Tabbie, eh?"

"Every day."

"And she is improving?"

"I believe so."

"And does she speak yet?"

"No, I am not emphasizing a regaining of speech to her. Right now I'm simply trying to create around her a world she will like and will want to come back to, with things that are simple and appealing to a child her age."

"Much trauma in her little life, yes?"

"Yes."

"She was bi-lingual as are all Latino children in this country. And smart like her father. Her mother now—she was another thing."

"Another thing?"

"Ah yes. Not a good mother. Many parties. Many lovers."

"And was Mr. Ron that way also?"

"I think not. He always busy. Make money. Little Latino boy from the other side of the tracks makes good, eh? But you do good thing to work with Tabbie."

"I hope so."

"Let us know when she speaks again. We will celebrate! Well, I go now, but I will see you for Fiesta, eh?"

"Yes. I am planning to be there."

"I will see you then. Remember you are my date."

"Oh yes," I smiled, but inwardly I was trying not to be resentful of Loro's date with Ron for the fiesta. I was discovering that she was showing the same kind of persistence, as I had been known to have. Again, I admonished myself sternly—he was my employer, nothing more. The conflicting feelings he roused were too difficult to deal with.

Besides, Luis might be fun—I had heard that he was an excellent dancer and that he had a playful sense of humor.

That evening at supper I happened to mention Luis' visit.

"What was he doing over here?" Ron asked

"Just a casual visit. He asked about Tabbie—if she is getting better."

"I don't particularly like his being here."

"Oh?"

"So don't encourage him to hang around."

"Ron, I was not encouraging him. I had not seen him since we visited the Señora, until he turned up on the patio this afternoon during Tabbie's naptime."

"All of the Fuentes are welcome here...but..."

Maria who had come in to pass dishes spoke up. "But he hung around too much when Cara was here, no? Ron, you should tell Gail the truth."

"Oh, I see. I'm sorry," I said.

"Just so you know," Maria said. Ron said nothing, but rose and left the room.

The days had fallen into a pleasant pattern. Mornings Tabbie and I would spend a couple of hours doing educational board games, reading, and finger painting. We would take walks around the yard and I would point out flowers, tell her their names, and the names of trees on the estate. She still did not speak, but I knew now that she was listening, because she would point at flowers and trees we had discussed and smile. Often we would walk along the beach followed by the puppy who was rapidly turning into a dog, and whom Tabbie adored.

She also adored the water and grew bold as the days went by, flirting with the waves and dodging in and out with their movement. On days when the water was calm, we wore bathing suits under our shorts and she would wade in the shallows. She became well acquainted with anemones, shells, and pebbles, which we spent a great deal of time collecting and examining. Sometimes she would take a little pail and shovel, and dig holes and make sand castles.

One time she filled her pail with pebbles and shells, and that evening at the supper table she gave them to her father to admire. He glanced at them with a puzzled expression, and I realized that he was going to return them with no comment, and intervened.

"They are really quite pretty shells and pebbles. Tabbie picked them especially for you. Wouldn't you like to take a look at them?"

He took time to carefully examine and mutter how very fine each was. Afterwards she was smiling from ear to ear and he coaxed a kiss from her.

On our trips to the beach, I would sometimes swim a little, enjoying the brisk cold water and air. Or, I would take Tabbie in my arms and wade into a deeper part so she could get used to it and feel secure. Little by little, I began to teach her to swim, and when she was able to paddle several strokes, I would catch her up and tell her how proud I was of her.

During our morning lessons I often read her Bible stories—Daniel in the Lion's Den, David and Goliath, Jonah and the whale, Jesus and the Samaritan woman. After our morning lessons we would have cookies and milk, and bow our heads and say grace, a little ritual she particularly loved.

Ron was often absent during the evening meal, working late, or making trips to his ranch in the mountains, and soon Tabbie was bowing her head before the evening meal and waiting for grace to be said. I knew it would not be long before she would do this when her father was present, and I was not wrong. He started eating, and then stopped, when he realized that Tabbie and I were not eating, and that Tabbie was waiting with bowed head.

"Are we giving thanks, Tabbie?" he asked. She nodded without raising her head. He bowed his head. "Please, Gail," he said, and I poured out a prayer of gratitude to God for His blessings. Afterward I thought I saw Ron brush away a tear, but I may have been mistaken. He was such a manly man...but then even manly men love their little daughters.

When she took her little pail and left he spoke. "You seem to have very effortlessly bonded with my daughter, Gail."

"She is easy to love and she knows I love her."

"But you love all little girls, do you not?"

"Most are quite lovable, but Tabbie is special."

Impulsively he reached over and covered my hand, which was resting on the table. Unexpectedly a shock wave climbed from my hand, up my arm, and lodged in the pit of my stomach. I raised my eyes to his face. He was looking at me intently. I quickly lowered my eyes and began to pull my hand away as a blush stung my cheekbones. Hastily, I rose. "Excuse me, I need to check on Tabbie," I said, and ran out so quickly I almost stumbled while rounding the chair at the end of the table.

Tabbie was playing in the patio under the sharp eyes of Ramón. I sat down in a patio chair to watch her and give myself a good scolding. "Fool", I said. "Fool."

I remembered one time when I was a child. I was asking my mother questions about the devil. "I bet he is really, really ugly," I said, "with horns, and tail, and red all over..."

My mother laughed. "How wrong you are, Honey. When Satan shows up he usually appears as the best looking, most beautiful, or handsomest thing yoi've ever seen. You see, Dear, Satan used to be a beautiful angel, very high in position in heaven. Then he became jealous of God, so he was demoted and thrown out of heaven. He can look any way he pleases. And usually he chooses to look very good!"

And Ron was a very attractive man. Was he Satan in disguise—a personal nemesis?

It was getting dark, near Tabbie's bedtime. She crawled into my lap and I began to tell her about catching lightning bugs in Alabama. Before I knew it, her little eyes closed, and she was asleep. As I rested my cheek on her dark curls, I knew I probably should leave Buenaventura. There were too many cross-currents—Señora Fuente, Loro, Luis, Ron Casabon, my own secret identity, and an attraction to my employer which distressed and surprised me. But looking down at the sleeping child in my arms I knew I could not leave her. She had captured my heart, along with someone else at Buenaventura. I knew, for better or worse, I had started down a road that I would see to the end.

As the date for the Señora's gala neared, I got out my only cocktail dress and looked it over with a critical eye. Finally, I put it on and went to the kitchen for a consultation with Maria.

"Would this do for Fiesta?" I asked.

"Oh, the dress is beautiful. But for Fiesta? No. You must go to town. You must shop. Every dress shop in town will have Fiesta dresses."

"Well, I shall have to borrow a car, I'm afraid. I'm saving to buy one, but it will take awhile. Do you think Mr. Ron would let me have a car next Saturday to shop?"

"Well, you will ask him. Tonight. After dinner. Never ask a man for a favor before he eats. He is tired and cross and will usually say no. After dinner you ask him."

So I waited until after dinner that evening, explained that I needed to do some shopping in town that coming weekend, and asked if I could borrow a car or if Ramón could drive me.

He looked at me thoughtfully. "Ah? You are going to run some errands for Maria or Tabbie?"

"No, it's personal. You see, I've never attended a fiesta before, and Maria tells me I need an appropriate dress."

"And you need transportation to town. For a dress for Fiesta. This presents a problem. You see, I'm a lawyer, and, of course I try to obey the law, I would be willing to bet you have no California driver's license."

"No, I'm afraid I do not...have had no time or way to get one, yet. I intend..."

"Intentions do not count."

"But Ramón could..."

"Ramón is going to be busy."

"Well, Sir," I said stiffly, "if that's the way it is..." I rose and put my napkin down by my plate.

"There is only one solution," he said quickly, "I must be your chauffeur."

"But I don't think..."

"There is no other way. We will go Saturday morning." He rose, laid his napkin on the table, gave me a small bow, a half grin with a raised eyebrow and left. I realized I had been had.

I remained standing at my place at the table, a little shaken, hesitating between frustration and joy.

CHAPTER V

He picked me up in his sporty Lexus convertible that Saturday morning and immediately turned away from the small town of Carpentaria and headed up the coast toward Santa Barbara.

"May I ask where we are going?"

"Where did you want to go?"

"I want to buy a dress for Fiesta. Maria says there are many for sale in Carpentaria."

"Bah. What does Maria know?"

I was silent. He waited a moment then said, "There are many more dress shops in Santa Barbara, and I thought you would enjoy seeing the lovely city and have a drive along the water. You do enjoy the water, do you not?"

"I love it."

"You are teaching Tabbie to swim, I hear."

"Yes, and she's taking to it like a little tadpole. Children of her age easily take to the water unless they have learned to fear it."

"I appreciate what you are doing for Tabbie. She is becoming a different little girl from the one you first saw a few weeks ago. You do not think she is autistic?"

"If it is autism, it is a mild case. I had rather think it is psychological shock brought on by the death of her mother. From the first day I saw her, I felt she is too aware of things going on around her to be autistic, even though she was building a world inside her head—which is sometimes the beginning of a mental or emotional illness."

"She was escaping to her own little world."

"Exactly. This one is difficult--for all of us. Young as she is, it all was becoming too much for her."

"I can understand that. Sometimes it is too much for me."

"Me, too."

"How are you bringing her back to this world?"

"With a lot of love, hugs, anemones, shells, pebbles, swimming, horseback riding, reading books, telling her Bible stories. Love calls us to the things of this world, Ron, not one constructed in our heads by fear, or neurosis, or frustrated desire."

"Love calls us to this world. I like that."

"It's not an original idea."

"All of my life I'm been reaching for something in the future. Maybe I should concentrate on this world."

I laughed. "We do not have a lot of choice. This world is really the only one which God has given us. Well, for now, anyway."

He took me to an exclusive shop in Santa Barbara where he was well known. It seems it had been Cara's favorite shop, and I tried to ignore the curious stares of the saleswomen. And they managed to curb their curiosity long enough to fit me into a truly beautiful dress, all blue and silver, fitted, well molded to the hips, and then flaring into three flounces. Ron insisted that I try it on and show him how it would look. I did, twirling in front of him like a fashion model.

"Oh," he said, his voice and eyes serious. Then he spoke in Spanish and I caught the world *"Querida"*—beloved, which made my heart beat faster, but which I pretended not to understand.

"Do you like it Ron?"

"Very much."

However, when I saw the price tag I immediately took off the dress and handed it back to the saleslady. "I'm sorry," I said. "This is out of my league. Do you have anything less expensive?"

"No, we are a very exclusive shop, Ma'am," she said, and departed the dressing room, with the dress. A few minutes later when I emerged, dressed, I found Ron waiting for me, with a package in hand.

"Ron, the dress..."

"Here is the dress." He pressed the package into my hands.

"You bought it for me?"

"It was my pleasure."

"No, Ron, you can't do that."

"Can't do? Why can't I do?"

"But why?"

"The pleasure of seeing a beautiful woman in a beautiful dress."

"I had rather you didn't"

"No, you do not understand. This is not for your rathers. It is for my rathers. And I had rather buy it and see you wear it." He took my arm and steered me out of the door and toward the car. "Now we are going to have lunch over that beautiful ocean you love so much."

The restaurant was on rocks extending over the ocean, a lovely, upscale place, and again Ron seemed well known there. I noticed the proprietors and waiters taking an unusual interest in me. Ron introduced me to the headwaiter, "My daughter's teacher, Miss Templeton." The man nodded and returned to the kitchen with a knowing look.

"I think you are doing too much for me, Ron. I don't believe...well, these people we are meeting seem to think I..."

"I thought we had gone through all that already, and decided I was doing it all for me."

"Oh, Ron, I don't want personal feelings to get mixed up in my profession. I am Tabbie's teacher, that's all. That's my job."

"That is all Tabbie is to you? A job?'

"You know that's not true. I love that little girl. I'd hate to leave her—ever!"

"Why would that be? For what reason would you have to leave her?"

"If things between you and me became improper, I could not stay. I would have to leave her."

"Even if I cared deeply for you?"

"I hope you care. I want us to be friends."

"And you? Do you care deeply for me?"

I gulped. "Yes, Ron. I do care. I care more than I want to care. But I am not ready for—things."

"I see." He took my hand, kissed it, and folded it in his. "What are you ready for, Querida?"

This time there was no mistaking the endearment. I waited a long moment, trying to sort out a tangle of thoughts. "I...you...you do not really know me...who I am..."

"Oh, is this true? You have a hidden personality I do not know? You are, perhaps a cat burglar, or a mafia woman? Or you have several husbands you have not told me about?"

In spite of myself I laughed. "Nothing so dramatic or interesting. What am I ready for? I am, to be truthful, not ready for love. I do not need love right now. Love can be very demanding, and I do not need love to interrupt a happiness and peace I have found at Buenaventura—with Tabbie, and..." I swallowed hard, again. "With you."

"The question remains. What are you ready for?"

"You asked me what it was all about, that afternoon at the Señora's..."

"And you will tell me?"

"What I am ready for is a friend."

He gave my hand a gentle squeeze. "Friends. If that is what you want, what you need, I will be your friend. Right now."

"Thank you."

"Now tell me what is troubling you."

"Can I trust you?"

"Do you have a dollar?"

"Yes."

"Give it to me." I took a dollar from my purse and handed it to him. "Now I am your lawyer. Whatever you tell me will be held in strict confidence."

I hesitated a few minutes to collect my thoughts and then began. "I was raised by Alfred and Goldie Templeton in Middleton, Alabama, Ron. They were wonderful people and they gave me a stable and happy childhood. My father died two years ago. Almost immediately, my mother, Goldie, found that she had cancer, and she was dead a year later. But before she died she told me that I had been adopted, something I had not known before, and she told me that my birth mother was Elfrida Costello Fuentes of Carpentaria, California."

"Ah. Things begin to become clear."

"After my mother died, I felt so completely alone. I never had any siblings—Goldie was unable to have children. I have many Alabama cousins, uncles, and aunts, but I still felt alone and so vulnerable. My parents left me a little money, and the home they also left me brings in rent money. Well, I made one of those wild, spur of the moment decisions to come to California and meet Señora Fuente. I made it here, but when I saw her home, La Fuente—so imposing, so forbidding—I walked away, and kept walking until I found my way down to the beach where you found me. I was trying to capture in watercolor all of the beauty, to have something to remember it by. I had decided I could not impose on my natural mother in her lovely home; it might disrupt her life completely. I decided I would quietly turn around and go back to Alabama, but be able to recall that beautiful setting within my watercolor. Then you came bursting into my life. And with the sprained ankle I had no choice. I could go nowhere."

"Good luck for me and Tabbie. But do you want to leave, Querida?"

"At first I was upset and confused. I didn't know what was happening—what God was doing. You were difficult. And at the beginning Tabbie was spoiled and impossible. But the first time I held her in my arms a peace came over me. I believe devoutly in prayer. I believe that was God's answer—His saying, "I have everything under control. It is all right. I want you to help this child.""

"For which I am very much in your debt."

"In His debt, Ron. I would have run like a scared rabbit if I had been able."

"You are so religious then?"

"I do not like that term. Being 'religious' doesn't quite cover it. I am a Christian and a believer. I love the Lord and He is very real to me."

"And, if I am interpreting this correctly, you do not have love affairs?"

"No, Ron. I do not have love affairs."

"You do know, Querida, that story you just told me makes you Latina. One of us."

I laughed. "So it does. I have yet to learn who my natural father was. He might be Eskimo or Chinese for all I know."

"Perhaps the Señora will tell you one day."

"I hope so. She did accept me. She was distressed when we met, but not rejecting. I had the feeling as we left that she accepted me, and was even proud of me."

"She knew who you are."

"Yes, that was evident."

"But Loro and Luis. I do not think they know."

"I believe not. I have the feeling she does not want her family to know. Did you know before I told you, Ron?"

"Not really. I was guessing. But I could not make up such a good story."

"A good story?"

"Good for me, even if troublesome for you. I find it hard to believe that God would send the perfect woman 3,000 miles to help my Tabbie. And to help me."

"Help you?"

"Yes. I believe I am in love with you, Querida."

"Oh, Ron. Please do not say that."

"Why not?"

"Because love inevitably brings many complications."

"I will handle the complications."

"Perhaps it is not love. Perhaps it is just the challenge of a young female residing in your house. I have heard that Latin men like such a challenge."

He scowled. "I am not sixteen, Querida. I have known sadness, happiness, love, marriage, disillusionment, disappointment, despair, tragedy..."

"You lost Cara tragically."

"Yes. I lost Cara."

"And you must miss her dreadfully. Perhaps I am temporarily filling that place in your mind and heart."

"Let me tell you about Cara, Querida. I was just out of law school when I met her. She was from an old family here on the coast, from old money. She was exceedingly beautiful, exceedingly spoiled, exceedingly unreachable to a Latino boy from the wrong side of the tracks. I wanted her like I wanted that Lexus out there—to show that I could have her, that I had arrived in life. Probably I wanted her more than I had ever wanted anything before her—she would prove to me who I was capable of being. I was surprised and elated when she accepted my proposal. She went to my head like a glass of rare wine. We had the wedding of the century—all of the best and richest were invited. I will not deny that being a part of her family helped me in a business way and financially. But afterward I worked like a Trojan to give her the life I was sure she deserved—Buenaventura, credit cards with no limits, etc. While I was working to make us a good life, Querida, I discovered all Cara wanted was a money tree so she could continue to live a very selfish Cara-centered life. She was not in love with me.

"Probably she was incapable of real love. I am well aware of her infidelities, which were many, and soon I realized that I was not in love with her. We had used each other. Then Cara was murdered, no doubt by one of her lovers, because I will tell you what is not generally known. She was pregnant and the child was not mine. She was dead then, and Tabbie was so affected emotionally."

"That was so sad for you, Ron."

"Yes. Well, I withdrew into work and depression, still driven by all of those demons of wanting the best because I was not sure I deserved the best. My life with Cara had been a sham. It had proven nothing to no one. Not even to me. More than that, I was suspected by the police—am still suspected—of having murdered her. The fact that she was pregnant with someone else's baby, the fact that we had not gotten along well for so many years, the fact it was well known that she was unfaithful all were against me. Such things can drive a man to murder. They provide excellent motivation. I knew the feeling. But I did not kill her.

"When you came into my life it was like sunshine after a long winter storm. I began to see that it is not what I achieve, but what I have become in life that is important. You have given me back something very important, something very valuable. You have helped recall me to life. You show me the ocean again as I knew it when a small child, as Tabbie sees it. You give me new eyes to see my child, the beauty of the world, the value of the friends who have stood by me."

"What a beautiful compliment you give me! But don't say you are in love with me. You made one dreadful mistake in marrying Cara for the wrong reasons. You are successful, but at what cost! You almost lost yourself."

"Oh I will say it, yes, and I do not think I am making a mistake. But, Querida, you have requested friendship only. You have told me you do not have love affairs. I respect and will continue to respect that. But you will come to love me someday. I am a very determined man."

"And I am a strong-willed woman. I will not allow you to rush into another mistake. And please don't forecast. That is frightening."

"You are frightened of me?"

"Not the way it sounds. No, I am frightened of me."

"Do not be." Our lunch was coming. I saw the waiter approach out of the corner of my eye. Ron again raised my hand, kissed it, smiled at me, and released it. I wrestled with the feeling I had been had—again.

Mexico must have picked the fifth of May as an appropriately beautiful day to fight for the victory of the Mexican army over the French in 1862, depose Archduke Maximilian of Austria as ruler, and, in the ensuing centuries, celebrate Mexican culture--food, music, beverage and customs unique to their country on that day! I kept Tabbie to her schedule, although my heart was racing with excitement at wearing my beautiful new dress, being with Ron, and seeing my birth mother again. Tabbie and I had our breakfast, walked on the beach, rode horses around the estate, and watched the comings and goings of delivery people bringing food, flowers and packages next door. After lunch I put Tabbie down for her nap, took my beautiful fiesta dress out of the closet and lay it on the bed so I could look at it.

We were to leave at five. By four I was already hearing the mariachi band next door. I dressed nervously and went downstairs to wait. For what, or whom, I was not sure. Luis or Ron? I waited nervously until Ron came from the master bedroom in the back, immaculate in the black suit of a Caballero, white ruffles cascading down the front of his shirt.

"Oh, Ron, you look so handsome!"

"And you look so beautiful!" he replied smiling.

"Thank you, Sir," I replied, twirling.

"We shall have to work on that," he said.

"Work on what?"

"Latina women do not say thank you for compliments. They accept them as their due, as they should."

"There is a lot to learn."

Maria, Sequestra, Ramón, and little José had come to the foyer to admire and give us advice. All but Sequestra, who would stay with Tabbie, would come to the fiesta later. We were about ready to walk out of the door when Maria ushered Lora and Luis in. My little sister looked truly lovely in aqua and white lace, and I noted with a certain amount of anxiety that her dress was similar to my own. As for Luis, he looked dashing—but not with Ron's solid masculinity. Luis was built along leaner and, one would say, more primitive lines. The term "hungry wolf" comes to mind, but that may have been a part of his charm, and he was charming.

He admired me with the appreciative frankness of the Hispanic male and bent to brush my hand with his lips rather than shaking it.

"We have the two most beautiful señoritas, do we not, Ron? What a pleasure to accompany Señorita Gail to her first fiesta."

Loro, meanwhile, was hugging Ron's arm and exclaiming over his costume. I took Luis' arm. "Are we ready, *Amigo*?" I asked

"He laughed with a show of his very white teeth. "Vamos, Señorita."

Casa de la Fuente was alive with light, movement, and the sound of the Mariachi band. Cars were pulling up to the entrance and disgorging beautiful people in colorful fiesta dress. A group of young women came squealing toward us, stopped, blinked, and then saw Loro behind me and swarmed around her. We left them there with Ron gently attempting to disengage his arm and move on, and Loro clinging to it as though for dear life.

At last, we came to Señora Fuente standing with her husband. I looked at him curiously, wondering if he could be my natural father, and deciding he could not. He was too different—short, iron gray hair, bespectacled, a bit heavyset, with the rather aloof preoccupied air of a banker or C.P.A. He looked at me with interest that I resembled Loro, but not interested enough to ask questions, and soon turned to others, nearby. I would have said he had a head for figures, but not too much imagination. I did not doubt, however, that he was Loro's father. There was something hard about both of them--a bit steely. Aside from that, I saw them later, dancing and talking together with a great deal of affection. In vain I searched my memory of biology 101 for what was dominant and what not in human genes.

When he had turned aside to talk to masculine friends, Señora Fuente plucked at my sleeve. "Can we talk together privately, Gail?" She led the way to the master bedroom, and turned and locked the door behind us. "I must know why you are in California."

"I came, originally, to see you, Señora. But I lost my nerve. I was going to return home when Ron met me on the beach. I sprained my ankle and was forced to stay."

"I must know. Did you come to torment me or get money?"

"I do not do such things," I said stiffly. "I have my own home and my own profession."

"Your parents who raised you. They were good to you?"

"The best."

"Oh, I am so glad. Is Goldie well?"

"Goldie died a few months ago. Cancer."

"Oh, I'm sorry. And Joseph, your father?"

"Also passed away. Over a year ago."

"Ah, let me guess. You found yourself alone, and came to California to find your birthmother."

"You are right. But please do not feel that you must take up the relationship if you do not wish to do so."

"You misinterpret me. I wish very much to do so. The better I know you the more I wish to do so, but I will admit there are problems. Ron mistook you for Loro and began to talk to you?"

"Yes. We became acquainted. And he was looking for a teacher for Tabbie, so I took the job."

"You came looking for your lost mother. I am glad that I am that mother. Hija, you are a daughter to make me proud. I am glad you came. You need me, and I am happy you do.

But you may not realize that I need you, too. It was the angels who arranged it. Thank God you are here."

"You are right, Madre," I said, and with tears in her eyes she reached over to embrace me.

"Gloriá a Jesús!"

"Yes, Praise to Jesus."

"We will talk more. Together. Privately." She squeezed my arm, and we returned to the others.

Luis met us. "Ah, there you are. Come my dear, much more people to meet, I think."

We made the round of the rooms and ended up by the swimming pool where a chef was barbecuing fajitas and brisket on a huge barbecue drum. Luis poured himself a glass of tequila and secured a glass of non-alcoholic punch for me.

We sat for a while by the pool and talked. Then the orchestra in the ballroom started playing a rumba and Luis asked me to dance. He turned out to be a wonderful dancer, improvising and putting humor and drama in his dancing. I was able to keep up with him—just barely. Soon another young woman broke in who was able to match him drama for drama and I gratefully sat down. I did not realize that Ron was standing behind me until he bent down to whisper in my ear. "Aren't you hungry, Querida? Let's go find something to eat."

We went back outside, filled our plates and wandered over to a garden arbor draped with bougainvillea and sat down inside.

"Well, Gail, you are celebrating your heritage for the first time. Are you enjoying the holiday?"

"Oh, so much! How did you get away from Loro? She is infatuated with you, you know."

He shrugged. "Puppy love. She will be going away to college soon. She is dancing, I believe with some of the young men who are classmates. You were talking to La Señora?"

"Yes. Oh Ron, I am so relieved. She does like me. When I told her my parents had been good to me she said, 'Praise to Jesus'. Is she a Christian?"

"Probably. According to your definition, I would say she is a 'born again Christian.' You have that in common with her, no?"

"Oh yes! And you, Ron, what are you?"

"Well, I am not a heathen. I believe in God. I was baptized in the church as a baby, but I'm afraid that I have not been back too often since."

"Will you allow me to take Tabbie to church?"

"I see no objection to that."

"Perhaps you would go with us sometimes?"

"I will think about it." He took my plate and went to return it. When he returned to the arbor he said matter-of-factly, "Querida, I want to kiss you, may I?"

"Ron, I..." but he pulled me to my feet, took me in his arms and sealed my protests with his lips. "Ron," I said, struggling to break free. But he clutched me in a tight hug. "Ron, this isn't...it probably isn't..." I said against his ear, but he was kissing me again. Suddenly the fight went out of me, and a wonderful peace came over me—the same peace I had felt when I had held Tabbie. I felt that I had traveled a great distance over a rough road, and was at last home, there in his arms. I lifted my arms to encircle him and return the kiss. It was long and passionate, and when it ended, he lay his cheek against mine for a long moment, and then took my hand to lead me back to the house.

"I thought born-again Christians were cold people, Querida!"

I thought about the great and passionate love affairs in the Bible and laughed. "How wrong you are, Querido. But this is too soon. You promised me time, Ron. There are things I must think about."

He grinned at me. "I had to have that kiss, but you may have all the time you desire. May I ask why you need time?"

"Love has to mean something to me, Ron. I would not want to drift into and out of your life. I could not bear for that to happen. I would not want to be your mistress."

"My mistress! Now there is an interesting idea! Rather intriguing really. I will tell you the truth, Gail. That never came to my mind. But now that you bring it up, it is tempting!"

We were passing a bush filled with large, red hibiscus. I pulled a couple of the hard, green buds and threw them at him, and then both of us began to laugh. He caught my hands and drew me to him. "What if I promise to be your friend, but once in a while we slip off somewhere and I kiss you?"

"And I kiss you back! As you said, most tempting. Not very wise, but tempting. Just remember your promise to give me time."

"Time granted." He smiled his beautiful white smile.

We went back to the dance floor and slow danced through a couple of numbers until we were pounced upon by Loro. "So there you are," she said, and glared at me. "It's high time I got to dance with my date." I smiled and yielded Ron and walked over to sit down. Then Señora came over and sat down by me.

"What is this?" she asked. "Is Ron in love with you?"

"Oh, Señora, I don't know. I'm so confused."

"And you are in love with him?"

"Señora, I..." I shrugged and remained silent.

"I think you are," she said.

"How do you know when I don't?"

"In your eyes. In his eyes. In the way you look at each other."

"Is it so evident?"

"Oh, indeed."

"Give me permission, Señora."

"Permission?"

"My parents are dead. I need someone to tell me what to do. If we are in love, is it the right thing? Perhaps he thinks he is in love because he is lonely, and has lost Cara. Perhaps he wants a permanent teacher or mother for Tabbie. Ron tells me you are a Christian, *Madre*. Would we be unequally yoked together? Is this God's will? Or a trap of Satan? You have known him much longer than I have. He is a very compelling man, but is he a good man?"

"A compelling man—oh yes! If I were twenty years younger, available, and could catch him, I would marry him myself. A Christian? I am not sure. It is wonderful that you are a Christian. I am so glad. But Ron's spirituality? It is something he must work out. I am excited that you and Ron are in love and fearful that you may hurt each other, as good as you both are. I love you both. Both of you have been recently through too much sadness. Have you prayed about this?"

"Yes, but probably not enough."

"He is a good man, Hija."

"I am glad you love him, Señora, but I am not sure your recommendation is a valid one. It's obvious you are prejudiced in his favor."

"With no reservations. He is the best."

"But some people say he killed Cara."

"I do not know who killed Cara. Sometimes she needed killing. She was not good to Ron. He was miserable—stayed away from home. Slept in his office or at his ranch. He made himself rich, yes, but at such a price! Tabbie hardly knew him before you came. I do not know who killed Cara. Many people had many things against her. But, whoever it was, it was not Ron."

"Thank you. I believe I am a little less confused."

"Gail, would you do something for me?"

"Of course. Name it."

"Please do not tell Luis, or Loro, or Jorge, my husband, about our relationship. Perhaps there will be a time when it will have to be known, but not yet. I have my reasons."

"You can trust me. I'll tell no one. However, Ron knows."

"Thank you. I trust you and Ron."

"I was so excited, Señora, to learn that you are a Christian!"

"And it is so wonderful to have an hija who is a Christian! My family has not been a source of much encouragement or happiness for me. I have only known the Lord for a couple of years. I did not raise Luis and Loro in the faith, much to my regret."

"Luis belongs to your husband by a former marriage?"

"Yes. Jorge was a widower when I married him."

"Where do you go to church?"

"A small community church not far away. Would you like to visit it with me? I'll be going tomorrow."

"Why yes, I would. I have been thinking about a church."

"Wonderful! I'll pick you up about ten thirty. Church starts at eleven."

That will be fine. But are you sure you are up to it with all you have had to do and this fiesta this night?"

"I need my church. There are things I am going through I need strength for. Yes, I'll be up to it, and, Hija, plan to have lunch with me. I know a lovely little tearoom where we can talk. We have so much to learn about each other."

It was getting late. I saw Ron kiss Loro on the cheek and leave her with a young, redheaded man who seemed eager to take charge of her. Ron came to us and spoke rapidly in Spanish to the Señora, thanking her for the lovely evening. And I heard her reply and say something about *iglesia*—church. "Señorita," he said to me, "I must take you home. You are going to church tomorrow with Elfrida, I understand."

Our walk home was silent, but we felt no need to talk. He kept me near his side and took my elbow once or twice to guide me over the rough spots. When we got to the door, before we entered the house, he once more took me in his arms and kissed me, but quickly released me, unlocked the door, opened it for me, and walked down the hall toward the master bedroom, while I climbed the stairs slowly to my room.

I woke Sequestra who was sleeping in Tabbie's room, and told her to go home. The family had their own ranch-style house on the property, but since Cara's death, Ron had given orders that Tabbie was never to be left alone. Tabbie, herself was sleeping peacefully, the dog, almost grown now to a size between a cocker spaniel and a lab, sleeping at the foot of her bed. I went to bed, but not to sleep. Those kisses kept playing over and over in my head. It was very late when I finally drifted off.

CHAPTER VI

There was first a low growl and then panicked barking from Andy. I woke and sat up in bed. Then I heard a wild shriek, which I recognized was Tabbie's. I was up in a moment and at her door, then stood for a bare second, frozen. A dark figure—I knew it was a man in a ski mask—had picked the child up. But Tabbie was hitting, kicking and screaming her wild shrieks. The dog was yapping and growling, pulling at his trouser leg. I dived into the fray, caught her under her arms and pulled, screaming, "Let her go! Let her go!" And then, "Ron, Ron, Ron!" For a moment, there was a rather awful tug-of-war, the child between us. And then we heard Ron's voice shouting and running footsteps coming up the stairs. Abruptly the man dropped his hold on Tabbie and turned to charge down the hall toward the back stairs, Andy just behind him.

Tabbie was hysterical, shaking and crying. I held her close to sooth her as Ron appeared at the door. "Who was that? What happened?"

"Someone tried to take Tabbie!"

He looked toward the back stairs and left, running in that direction, but he, and Andy were back in a few minutes. He switched on the light. "I lost him. Left by the back door. Even left it open. Are you hurt, Tabbie?" Somehow he had managed to put on a bathrobe over his pajamas. He reached toward her, and she reached for her father.

"The man, the man," she sobbed. He took her in his arms.

"Are you all right, Tabbiecita?" She snuggled to him and her sobs grew quieter as he sat down in the rocker, rocking her and soothing her in Spanish and English. "The bad man of her nightmares is gone. Daddy made him go away!"

As frightened and upset as I was, I noticed how tenderly he cuddled and soothed her. Since then I have learned that Hispanic boys, particularly in poorer families, are charged with the care of their smaller siblings, just as are the girls— something lacking in Anglo families. Ron had come from a poor family with several younger siblings. My other thought was that she had turned to him, and I realized that the frightening incident had clarified one thing for her—her father was not the "bad man" of her nightmares. If I still had doubts, it had helped clarify that for me, also. When she grew quieter he looked at me. "Are you all right, Querida?"

"Just frightened."

"Take her, then. I must go notify the police." He gave her to me and I sat down in the rocking chair, my cheek against her head and thanked God for her kicking and screaming—which at one time had been so distressing to Ron and me, and for the barking of Andy. Gradually she got quieter and began to suck her thumb. It was not until that point that I realized that she had spoken. "Tabbie, you said 'the man.' Did you know the man who tried to take you?" She hid her face in my chest and shook her head. Hallelujah! She had responded to my question. The frightening incident had an upside. It had shocked her back into awareness.

I cuddled and rocked her until I felt her little body begin to relax. I became aware that I had on nothing but a thin cotton nightgown and was barefooted, but I was unwilling to put her down, frightened that somehow that dark figure would reappear and grab her.

It seemed like hours, but it couldn't have been over fifteen minutes before Ron returned with two young policemen, and it was pretty plain that they were out of their depth. They filled out forms and made notes. Did we have any idea who might want to take the child? (No.) Were outside doors in the house kept locked? (Yes.) Who locked up at night? (Ron.) Did the servants have keys? (Yes.) Were bedroom doors kept locked? (No.)

While these questions were going on, I asked Ron to move Andy, who had taken over the bed, and I put the sleeping Tabbie down so I could get on some clothes, slipping out of the room as inconspicuously as possible, keeping my eyes down and ignoring the sudden appreciative silence from all three men. I knew there would be little chance of sleep for the rest of the night so I put on blue jeans and a sweater, slipped on some moccasins and returned to Tabbie's room.

"Would you gentlemen like some coffee?"

They stared at me. What? Alabama customs in California? Then Ron spoke. "Gail, I want you to stay here with Tabbie. I'll call Maria to make coffee."

"All right." When they left I lay down on the daybed Sequestra had vacated earlier and tried to rest, but there was too much going on in my head. I heard voices and footsteps below. More men's voices. Maria's. After about an hour I heard a knock and Maria called. It was barely daylight. Five o'clock. She didn't wait for an answer, but came inside with a cup of coffee for me. I sat up and turned on a small lamp on the bedside table.

"It is so terrible, no? We almost lose our baby. Who could do such a terrible thing?" She sat down by me and continued without waiting for an answer. "Does the bad man want money, do you think? He wants to take our Tabbie and wants Señor Ron to pay money to get Tabbie back? Or does someone hate Ron, or does he just want a little girl to do something terrible with? Why our Tabbie? She have too many sorrows already. Lose her mother. Almost lose her mind."

"Maria, it may not be all bad. It scared and shocked her so badly she actually said something."

"What did she say?"

"She just said, 'The man, the man.'"

Maria thought a minutes. "Why do you think she said 'the man'?"

"I wish I knew. Maria, she was so brave and strong. She screamed and yelled, kicked and hit. If it hadn't been for all of that, I might not have wakened and run to her."

"You saw him?"

"With just the dim light from the hall outside. We wrestled over her. Had a tug of war and I won. I screamed for Ron and he came running up the stairs. I guess the man heard him because he dropped his hold on Tabbie and ran down the back stairs."

"¡Gracias a Dios!"

"Si," I said, without thinking. Someone was coming up the stairs. Ron entered with an older man whom I correctly judged to be a detective.

"Detective Milo, this is Miss Templeton, Tabbie's teacher. Maria, stay with Tabitha, please. Mr. Milo would like to speak to Gail downstairs."

The detective's keen eyes swept around the room, taking in the bed, the sleeping child, the dog at her feet, the furniture, the doors, the windows, the placement of the furniture, evaluating, measuring.

Ron escorted me out of the room. "Are you all right, Querida?"

"Yes, I'm all right. Just so relieved that Tabbie is okay. Oh Ron, if he had taken her! If we had lost her! I had to grab her. He was taking her out of the room."

"I owe you big time, Querida. If it were not for you he might have gotten away with her."

"Well, give credit to Andy, who first woke me with his barking and growling. And Tabbie, herself, who was putting up a magnificent fight."

"That dog has a lifetime ticket to anything he wants, and you and Tabbie are great fighters. I will be careful not to take on the two of you at one time."

When we got downstairs Ron had another police officer to talk to, and I went into the dining room, poured myself a second cup of coffee and sat down to wait. Presently Detective Milo came downstairs and into the room, pulling notes out of his pocket as he sat down.

"You saw the perpetrator, Miss Templeton?"

"Unfortunately just a dark shadow. I was awakened out of a sound sleep by Tabbie's screaming. It was about 3:30. I ran to her room and saw a dark figure with Tabbie in his arms. She was screaming and fighting. I got hold of her and there was brief tug of war. I was yelling for Ron, who sleeps downstairs, and when the man—the perpetrator—heard him running up the stairs he took his hands off Tabbie and ran toward the back stairs."

"You did not turn on the light?"

"No. We had our little wrestle in the dark."

"You were able to tell it was a man, not a woman?"

"Hmmm. I had not considered that it might be a woman, but I believe it was a man. He was taller than most women, and because of his strength and the fact he moved like a man. At one point Tabbie kicked him in the stomach and he grunted. It was a man's grunt."

"A young man or an old man?"

'A young man. A young punk man."

"Why do you say 'punk'?"

"Punks are wiry, quick-moving, quick on their feet. At least that is my impression of punks."

"Interesting. And you believe this man was like that?"

"Yes."

"You did not see his face?"

"He was wearing something like a ski mask or stocking over his face."

"What else?"

"Black, long-sleeved, pullover shirt. Black trousers."

"Black or dark-colored?"

"There was no light to see by. It could have been either."

"I see. Are you new to this area, Miss Templeton?"

"I've been in California only a few months."

"How did you get your present position?"

"Quite by accident. Mr. Casabon was looking for a teacher for his daughter, who is having problems since her mother died. We became acquainted, he learned of my credentials, and hired me."

"Heard how?"

"I told him, and he checked."

"So how did you meet?"

This was getting sticky. Would I have to reveal the facts of my birth? And what about the Señora? I could not reveal her secrets. To my relief Ron appeared at the door.

"I can answer for Miss Templeton. I am her lawyer. Our meeting was accidental. She was on the beach, doing some watercolor, I believe. As you can see, she is very attractive. I spoke to her and we began to talk. I was lucky enough to need a teacher for Tabbie, and she has excellent credentials, as you will discover when you check her out."

"And why would Miss Templeton need a lawyer?" Milo asked.

"Some personal matters which have nothing to do with this case."

He asked a few more questions under Ron's careful gaze and I escaped to the kitchen, Ron following. Tabbie was eating cereal at the breakfast bar and Maria and Sequestra were busy making breakfast taquitos. Careless of them, he stopped and took me in his arms. "Ron..."

"Shhh, Querida." He just held me. Then I saw the wisdom in that moment and just held him. In a few minutes, he released me and I looked up to see him smiling. "And what are you grinning at, Sequestra? I saw you peeking at us."

Sequestra only laughed and looked away. "Ha!" Maria said, "You think you fool us. We know all the time."

I went to Tabbie and hugged her, but she was busy with her cereal, evidently having been able to forget and put behind her the events of the night. Ron caught my hand again and led me to the door. "Let's go for a little walk, Querida."

We walked out into another beautiful California day, hand-in-hand toward the ocean. At last, he stopped and faced me. "Querida, at this point it may be very good for the police and everyone else to think we are lovers. Less suspicious."

"Less suspicious for...?"

"That you would be working with anyone to take Tabitha."

"What?" My first reaction was pure anger. "Ron, how dare you! That such a thought would cross your mind!"

"Querida, it is not me. Couldn't you see where the detective's questions were heading?"

"No, no, Ron!"

"Yes, Gail. Yes, Querida. He will check you out thoroughly, but he will find nothing of interest in this case. I have already checked before I would let you take charge of Tabbie."

"You didn't find out about my birth records."

"No. I saw no reason to go back that far. I do not think they will, unless, well, unless they find out about the resemblance between you and Loro. The police have strong doubts about such coincidences. They may check that out."

"Oh Ron!" I sat down on the grass and took my head in my hands. He squatted beside me in that effortless squat at which western men seem so adept.

He reached over to put a lock of hair behind my ear. "Welcome to my world, Querida. We are not in Alabama anymore."

"You...you don't think that, do you Ron? That I'm somehow involved in a plot against you?"

"No," he said gently. "Not at all. And, you, do you believe in me?"

"Yes." I said, but tears began to seep from under my eyelids.

"You regret coming to Buenaventura? You wish to return to Alabama?"

"I just wish not to have this trouble." I yelled. "I wish I could go home!"

"Is it that the smart Christian lady from a fine, upstanding family in the Southern United States would not want to be the Querida of the Latino boy from the wrong side of the tracks, who brings trouble?"

"It's just that I was just beginning to establish a relationship with the Señora! I promised her I would tell no one. She especially requested that we do not tell, particularly her family."

"Have you noticed, Querida, for each victory, there is often new trouble? I'm sorry I brought this on you. I know how depressing suspicion can be."

"And what is next for you, Querido? What is next for Buenaventura? Will any of this suspicion concerning last night's incident affect you adversely?"

"Two violent incidents in such a short time is not good. Yes, it will probably make it harder for me. But I need to know, with all of this, are you still my Beloved? My Querida?"

I put my head in my hands and hid my face. Trouble had invaded my paradise. Briefly, thoughts of my peaceful home in Middleton, the giant oaks and magnolias that surrounded it came to mind. My aunts and cousins and the wonderful holiday feasts at their farm, Christmas, Easter egg hunts, births, weddings, and anniversary celebrations to enjoy. My heart ached with longing to see them again.

But what of Ron? Could I leave him and Tabitha? No. I loved them too much. I realized suddenly that I had always had an advantage solidly at my back—my father and mother, their support and care. Like all children, I had taken that as my due. Now I was invited to step back and give, rather than take. Could I accept blame and suspicion? Could I sacrifice when it was not for just me? If not, I had no right to Buenaventura, to the love of and for Ron and Tabitha.

Then one of those wonderful incidents that happen occasionally in the Christian's life took place. "Where is your faith, Gail?" a voice inside me asked. "Where is your courage? All of your life you have benefited from the love and work and sacrifices of others—the parents who raised you. The Señora who gave you life, and then gave you up because she loved you. And now the man beside you who has shared his home, his child, his life, his heart with you. Open your eyes and look around. Is it worth fighting for?" I knew it was God speaking. The moments passed in silence as I allowed peace to come over me.

Finally, I raised my head and looked at Ron's worried face. "Don't you even suspect how much I love you, Ron?"

He flashed that smile like a burst of sunlight. "You do, Querida?"

"Oh, yes. Yes, indeed. From the first moment we rolled down the cliff together.'"

"You are not afraid of tarnishing that spotless, born-again image?"

"Good Christians don't run away from trouble, Querido." He pulled me to my feet and kissed me and we walked back to the house with our arms around each other. "Ron, while you and your amigos teach me Spanish, I must begin the laborious task of teaching you Southern United States English. Repeat after me 'hissy fit'—accent on the first syllable, as in many Spanish words..."

"Hissy fit," he said matter-of-factly.

"That's good. Perfect."

"And it means?"

"A type of tantrum. Usually confined to children of Tabitha's age and American teen-agers. But occasionally straying into the adult agenda."

"It's good to know the finer nuances of the English language. Am I to understand...?"

"You are to understand nothing. We will not go there. The agenda of *all* adults, including Hispanic males..."

He squeezed me. "Not so, Querida!"

"Ah, but so. However, charitably, we will not go there either. Another Southern USA phrase—an old Alabama phrase my father used when I would tell him of some difficulty in my life. He would say, 'We are going to lick this sucker, Sweetheart.' And that is what I am saying to you. We're going to lick this sucker."

He laughed. "I believe I like Alabama phrases."

"This trouble—we are going to lick it. The mystery will be solved. I will not have it hanging over our heads, or over Tabbie's head for the rest of her life. We will find out who murdered Cara, and they will pay. And I believe it is connected to last night's incident."

"Gail, you are not to go looking for murderers."

I don't think we will have to look, Querido. I believe he will come to us and we will find him out. He has to pay for what he has done to Cara, what he has done to Tabbie, and to you. He showed us last night that he will not quit. Whether we look for him or not he will find us. And when he does, we will have him!"

"You give me courage, Querida. By the way, you look most tempting in your nightgown."

"Hmmm. Should I say thank you?"

"Not required. You look like a blonde Madonna when you hold the child. Which reminds me…the Señora will be expecting you to go to church with her. I think you should go. It will get you out of the house until the police leave."

"Probably a good idea. I need a quiet place. I need to talk to God."

"Talk to Him for me, too, Querida."

"Will do," I grinned, stood on tiptoe and kissed him.

CHAPTER VII

The phone was ringing when we returned to the house, and it was the Señora asking for me.

"Gail, I see police cars at your house. Is something wrong?" she asked.

"Yes, Señora. Are we going to church?"

"Yes, if you are able to get away."

"I'll tell you on the way to church. Señora, do me a favor, will you?"

"Of course."

"Please do not let Loro come to the house."

"This does not concern Loro?" There was alarm in her voice.

"No, not at all. I'll tell you about it."

A pause. "I'll pick you up presently."

"Thank you, Señora."

"I was beginning to feel the weight of the night—all of it, fiesta, Ron's kiss, my tussle with the intruder who almost took Tabbie, the lack of sleep and too much expenditure of energy, not to mention my near "hissy fit" and finally telling Ron I loved him.

When had I first began to love him? When I saw his silhouette astride his horse against the sky? When he shouted at me in words that confused me? When he leaped on the rock and onto the beach, taking me with him? When he rolled over my body to protect me from falling rocks? Or was it when he lifted me to the horse and I felt his hands, warm and capable? Or perhaps when he shouted at me with eyes like black marbles when he thought I was mistreating his daughter? Or when Loro snubbed me, and took his arm and led him away, leaving me in tears?

Or was it when he played word games with me? Tricking me into letting him take me to Santa Barbara, buying me the fiesta dress? (Lord, I love that dress!) His rathers, he had said, not my rathers. The "smart Christian lady" outwitted by the "Latino from across the tracks!" I smiled.

I drew myself a tub full of water as hot as I could stand it, sprinkled it with bath salts, and climbed in. If anything would get me through the rest of the day, this would be it.

I lay back, remembering the way he had frolicked with his daughter on the beach, sending her into gales of giggles, splashing her with water, and pretending to be chased in return—helping to open a new world to Tabitha. To himself. To me.

And when he would not allow the Señora to interview me alone, but had firmly insisted on coming. His protection, again, for both the Señora and me, when the police had begun to ask too many questions. His face—dear, worried, apprehensive—as he asked me if I would stay, would be his "Querida" instead of running back to Alabama. No anger, just a calm waiting. Oh, Ron!

I closed my eyes for a moment, then looked at my watch and sighed. It was now or never if I was going to get on with my life. I climbed out of the tub, feeling a little better. Not quite ready to climb a new mountain, but I would fake it. What will love call us to do now, dear Lord?

"Why are the police here, Hija?" the Señora asked, as soon as I was in the car.

"We had an incident last night, Madre. Someone tried to take Tabitha from her bed."

"Oh no!"

"Yes. If it were not for the child's screams he would have succeeded."

"Was he seen?"

"Tabitha sleeps in the room next to me. There is an adjoining door between the two rooms. I got a brief glimpse of him, but of course it was dark."

"What time?"

"Probably about three thirty."

"But why would someone try to take Tabitha? For ransom money, perhaps?"

"Perhaps, but I rather think it has something to do with that previous incident. With Cara's death."

"We still do not know that was not an accident!"

"Ron suspects that it was not. Let's face it, I did not know the lady, but from what I've heard she had an unsavory reputation. Cara had lovers. It could have been one of them.

She neglected Tabbie and Ron. Slept around. Who knows what she was into? Señora, would you know—was she doing drugs?"

She waited a moment too long to answer, shock in her face. "No. Well, I don't know. I had not considered that. But that is a possibility isn't it?"

"Yes, among others."

"You mentioned Loro...?"

"The police suspect everyone, of course. They are wondering why I came here from Alabama, and I promised you I would keep our relationship a secret. But if they see Loro, they are going to wonder why we look so much alike and why we both look so much like you. Ron says that they—the police—do not believe in coincidences, and they may look into my background."

"Oh, Gail, no! That would be very difficult for me. You see, I have never told Jorge. He is from the old school. I'm not sure that he would ever forgive me if he learned about it."

"I am sorry." For a moment I wanted to add, "The matter of my birth has been difficult for me, too." But I didn't. Still, it hurt that the Señora would think of me in that negative way. "Ron will do everything possible to keep that information from getting out."

"I know he will. But we can't trust Loro. I told her when I left to stay away from Buenaventura. However, from pure contrariness, especially if she sees the police cars, she may go over. I can't control her...her father does better than I. A little better, that is."

"She's still a teen-ager."

"Yes, and she has been in love with Ron since she was ten."

"He calls it puppy love."

"I don't know if it is puppy love. It's lasted a long time. For this reason she doesn't like you very much. But forgive her."

"Did she dislike Cara, also?"

"No, she idolized Cara. She was much younger then, of course."

"Not a good model."

She sighed. "I know. I know."

We had arrived at the church. It was a small church, tan brick with a modern version of a spire at the top. The windows were brightly stained glass. The benches were white with mauve carpeting. Behind the pulpit was a large reproduction of Holman's Head of Christ, framed in gold. The atmosphere was reverent but lighthearted. Several people, already seated looked up and smiled. I liked the church and immediately felt at home. I was happy to see that it had a prayer room, which was open much of the time. With all that was happening, the events that were taking place so fast in my life, it was nice to know there was a place where I could get away and pray.

The minister was young, boyish, and sincere. His sermon was about Jesus as the Good Shepherd, how the Lord watches over His own, and will lead us to still waters in time of trial. I needed that sermon, and I was feeling better when it was time to leave. On the way out several Hispanic women surrounded the Señora and chatted happily in Spanish. She switched to English and introduced me as "a relative from Alabama." They, also, switched to English and exclaimed how very much I looked like Loro, and would I be making my home in Carpentaria? I told them that "at this time, it is a visit only," and they seemed sincerely disappointed. Somehow, I was, too. Was I recognizing that sooner or later my time with Tabbie, with Ron and the Señora would be up and I would have to leave?

I knew that, for Ron, perhaps my declaration of love for him, was the end of a journey. I knew only that I could not hide my love for him any longer, that it was out in the open, known. Ron had not asked me to marry him, and as I had told him, I did not have affairs. What if he should ask me to marry him? There was that troublesome verse from the Apostle "Be not unequally yoked together." It was that verse, as much as the fact that I had wanted to keep the employer-employee relationship on a business basis, which had led me all along to try to keep that distance between us. Why didn't I simply ask him to make a profession of faith, and become a true Christian? I could give Ron an ultimatum—"Accept Christ, or you don't get me." But that was kind of like putting my value above the Lord's. In addition, if Ron did accept Christ just to please me, would that acceptance have any real value? No, he would have to establish his own relationship with the Master.

To a non-Christian man in love it would be easy to say it was not important. We would deal with it later, etc. etc. But I could not do this halfhearted Christianity. My parents had warned me, and I had seen it lived out in the lives of friends, halfhearted Christianity led to chaos. Eventually, down the road, there would be big trouble as values clashed.

Moreover, the attraction between us was too strong; we would not be able to live together at Buenaventura without having to battle that attraction day and night.

As we pulled out of the parking lot, the Señora put her hand on my arm. "We will go to lunch, Gail? There is much we need to talk about alone."

"Yes, I agree." I called Ron on her cell phone to tell him our return would be delayed. She drove us to a lovely tearoom in a mall in the suburbs of Santa Barbara. We ordered crepes and salad, and then she sat back and gave a sigh.

"There are questions you would like to ask me?"

"Many."

"Should I just tell you the story?"

"Please."

She waited a minute, then sighed again, put her napkin in her lap and leaned back in her chair. "You have to understand, Hija, that I was raised in a very strict and proper family. These days young people do not know about strict and proper. I do not think, Gail, that you know much about Mexican customs?"

"I did not even know I was Mexican until last year, and I found out then purely by chance."

"It means so much to me that you had a good childhood. My conscience has tormented me about that. I felt that I could trust Goldie and Joseph, but a mother always worries.

They were such good people and they wanted a child so much."

"They loved me, were good to me."

"It would have been so very different if I had kept you, tried to raise you. My father would have insisted that we raise you as I was raised. Those old Mexican customs have largely fallen by the wayside, thank God, but my father was a member of the old school. As a teen-ager I went to private, parochial girls' schools, and was not allowed to date in high school, was not allowed to wear makeup, and I wore my hair in a bun at the back. My family was a part of an old Latin enclave in Santa Barbara, and I was expected to marry within that group when it came time to marry. My father had always been a cold man, but after I had you he was especially cold. He would have been the same, or worse, to you, if I had brought you home with me. I was not allowed to return to college. I was virtually under house arrest.

"And then one day a few years after you had come and gone, a wealthy widower, a business acquaintance of my father came to our house and noticed me. He asked my father if he could ask me out. My father agreed. By then he had come to realize that I was not an asset to him or the family, and that something should be done or he would have me on his hands for the rest of his life. He admonished everyone not to breathe a word to anyone about my earlier lack of judgment, and, to make a long story short, I eventually married Jorge Fuente.

"But it has not been a marriage made in heaven. Jorge is a duplicate of my father. Why is it, Hija, that people so often marry a personality exactly like the difficult family member they are trying to get away from? Is it God making us face the same situation over and over until we can follow His directions and master it? At any rate, Jorge was difficult to begin with, and has gotten more difficult with the years. His redeeming feature is that he loves his children—Luis and Loro, but I do not know what he would do if he were told you are my daughter!"

"He is abusive?"

She quickly looked away. "He was not at the beginning. I had comparative freedom, but through the years he has grown colder and more distant, began to get verbally abusive, to me, and to a lesser degree to the children, especially Luis. Lately it has gotten worse.

"Of course I was not in love with him, nor he with me. Jorge needed an attractive, well-bred wife to act as hostess at home and mother his children. And me? I was never in love with anyone but your natural father."

"Tell me about him."

"Yes. It's a great relief to talk to someone about it after all of these years. As I told you, my life at home was very restricted. Growing up I could be with boys only if a chaperone was present. I went to a convent school—all girls. My knowledge about love and sex were *nada*—nothing. I graduated high school early—I was only seventeen, but I was at the head of my class, and I was offered a scholarship to a local university. My father was persuaded to let me go— against what he called his 'better judgment,' as he would remind me often through the years. The university and the freedom it brought me were heady stuff. I found new friends—both young women and young men. I met Goldie, and we became close, though she was a few years older than I was, and married. She used to compare notes with me about literature—both of our majors, and she was a wonderful help when I was preparing an essay or studying for an exam.

"There was a group of young Chilean air cadets who were in training to be pilots at a nearby air station. They would come to Santa Barbara when they were on leave, sometimes to our campus where there were young men and women their own age. Many of us spoke Spanish, their native language, and we became friends with them.

"I met him in the Student Union. His name was Roberto Reed."

"My natural father?"

"Yes.

"But that is not a Hispanic name!"

"No. His father was an English diplomat, stationed in Chile, who had spent many years there, and married a Chilean wife. Roberto was not a tall man, but he was extremely good looking, a young god to me. He was under six feet, with blue eyes and a fair complexion. I was attracted to him the first time I ever saw him, as I believe he was to me. We spent a great deal of time in groups of young people, stealing looks at each other. Finally he got up the nerve to talk to me, and later I got up the nerve to ask him to a student function—a play by the drama department, I believe it was. He accepted, and we were together often after that, whenever he could get leave. We had a great deal in common. He was bi-lingual, as I was, and was fascinated with the fact I was studying English literature, which we often discussed. He had a lively mind, and a good sense of humor, and was, in every sense, a gentleman—until. But anyway, one night he kissed me!"

"And such a kiss to a seventeen-year-old girl who has had no masculine attention or appreciation during her lifetime is a bombshell!"

"How well you know your psychology, Hija. It was indeed. How easily a man can make a fool of a woman!"

"Or it can be the other way—a woman can make a fool of a man."

"Perhaps we are all fools if we are really in love."

"Such tricks nature plays on us!"

"A subject for much theological surmise and debate. Well, using no sense in anything but the need to have that young man, I discovered love. We were together two, or maybe three times, and then he just, well, disappeared!"

"Disappeared?"

"Yes. He simply vanished from my life."

"Oh, what a disaster!"

"It was indeed. Finally some of the other young men from his squadron told me that he had finished his tour of duty in the states and been returned to Chile, and that he had a sweetheart there who was awaiting him.

"I thought it was impossible. I thought it could not happen. Then I found that I was pregnant. I kept hoping and praying that I would get a card, a letter, anything to let me know he cared. I had dreams of flying to Chile to marry him, spending a lifetime with him in that interesting country. But it was not to be. And I had to tell my parents with the resulting consequences." She stopped speaking and spent a few minutes lost in thought. The waiter came with our orders, we spent a few minutes in silent prayer and then began to eat.

"I am deeply sorry you had to go through these things, Madre."

"No one to blame, Hija, but my own foolish self."

"So that was my birth father—son of an English diplomat and a Chilean woman, a young air cadet on a tour of duty in the United States. Really, Madre, it is a romantic and beautiful story, a pure love between two innocents. I believe the reason you never heard from him was that he had real feelings for you, and he did not trust himself to contact you again. He was expected to return to Chile and resume his life there, with someone his parents no doubt approved of. He never knew you had his child?"

"No. When I told my parents and my father isolated me. I was not allowed to contact any of the students or the Chilean cadets again, with the exception of Goldie, who was older and a married woman. Goldie's husband was in the navy stationed in Santa Barbara, and she was filling her time waiting for him by taking some graduate courses. She wanted to be a college teacher, I remember."

"Yes, she taught in a local college for many years before she died."

"I am so glad she was able to fill that ambition. Well, to return to my story, when her husband came home on leave, they asked me if they could adopt the baby, and I was old enough then to be able to choose and give my consent. That angered my father. He said a Mexican baby should stay in a Mexican family, but I knew you would not have had a happy life if I had kept you.

"Thank you, and thank you for telling me the story. That is a sacrifice I can never repay."

"You have already repaid by accepting me, letting me be a madre to you, letting me confide things I have never been able to tell anyone before. I have had to keep silent so long."

"You say your life still is not peaceful, that Jorge is becoming increasingly difficult."

"Yes, I believe something is going on in his life that he will not or cannot tell me. I suspect that it may have something to do with money. Of course, he never tells me what sort of shape our finances are in. I knew he lost some money not long ago on some worthless stock that went down instead of up. Even after that happened, he bought the plane to make his trips to Mexico and Central America. He said he needed it for his import-export business. Ron had warned him about that stock—Ron is very good with money. But Jorge would not listen."

"But the fiesta—I know that must have been very costly."

She shrugged. "The Cinco de Mayo festival held at our house is a tradition in Carpentaria. We held the first one to celebrate Loro's arrival. Even if I wanted to cancel it now, I could not because Loro and Jorge would not let me. That stubborn Spanish pride. Everyone would know Jorge has money problems, which would be a humiliation for him in his circles. Hija, are you going to marry Ron?"

"He has not asked me to marry him."

"But he will. I can see it in his eyes, in the way he looks at you. He is very much in love with you."

"What can I say, Madre? He is not a Christian!"

The Señora leaned her head on her hand and shook it. "Ah, the instructions of the Old Apostle, not to be unequally yoked! Why must life be so difficult?"

"I wish I knew." I felt tears rising in my eyes.

"You love him, Hija?"

"Yes, yes. Oh, yes." The waiter came, took away our plates, and brought dessert—a dainty soufflé of some sort. I sat and looked at it. Then picked up a spoon, determined to sidetrack the tears and do the dessert justice, but I felt a few spill over on my cheeks, even so. The Señora opened her purse, took out a dainty lacy, perfumed handkerchief and handed it to me.

"Thank you."

"It is my pleasure. I didn't get to kiss little bruises and punctured fingers when you were growing up, but this helps to make up for it, for me."

"And me too," I said, wiping my nose and smiling. "And I love Tabbie. I don't want to leave her—him—either of them. Tabbie is just beginning to come back to life. Did I tell you she spoke a little after the incident last night?"

"No, you didn't! What did she say?"

"She just said, 'The man, Daddy, the man!' and she was clinging to her daddy and crying."

The Señora put down her spoon and stared into the distance for a moment. "'The man'. Hija, could she have seen the person who murdered her mother?"

The idea shot through me like an electric bolt. "Of course, Señora! That would make sense. Often she will become very quiet and go to the window and look out toward that place where Cara was killed. That would be why he was trying to take her! He was going to kill her because he was afraid she would regain speech and identify him! If we are right, Señora, she is in a great deal of danger."

"If I know her father he will watch her like a hawk," the Señora said. "It was good the incident took place, because that has put us on alert. We must tell the police and Ron." She saw me putting my napkin down and picking up my purse. "Wait, I am not quite ready to go yet. You were talking about leaving Ron and Tabbie. I'm afraid it would be disastrous for both of them."

"Yes. She has already lost one mother—two times. The first when Cara was too busy with high living to be a mother to her, the second when she was killed and Tabbie lost her permanently. And Ron—he was not there for Tabbie either. Man-like he simply buried himself in his work."

"You are talking about Tabbie, and I agree with you, but I said it would be disastrous for both of them. Have you thought of the harm it would do to Ron?"

"I don't want to think about that. I don't want to hurt Ron," I said feeling the tears beginning again.

"And there is another wonderful human being who would be heartbroken, and that is Gail. Not to mention her Madre. My heart would also break for all three of you, whom I love very much. We will pray this bad thing will not happen. Please count the cost, Hija."

"Thank you, Madre," I said, wiping my eyes again. "And I owe you prayers also. I will always keep your confidence. Ron knows, but he's my lawyer, bound my law not to tell, although he wouldn't any way."

"Your lawyer? How did that happen?"

"I needed someone to confide in. He made me give him a dollar, and then told me I was his client and everything I told him would be kept in confidence."

She laughed. "Oh Hija, be careful of him. He is a clever man! So that is the way he wormed our secrets out of you? And, confiding in him, you opened your heart to him!"

"I'm afraid so. I see it now, I've been had, and not just once, but several times." The tears were gone, now and we were laughing together. We dawdled over dessert for another hour, laughing again and again as I told her other stories of Ron's outwitting me, and we both began to appreciate what a very good lawyer he was, and why he had become extremely wealthy. Then the Señora told me stories of Luis and Loro's growing up, and I told her of funny ups and downs in my childhood. We were not only mother and daughter; we were best friends when we parted.

When I arrived back at Buenaventura, I found the police had departed, but chaos reigned. In the kitchen, I heard Sequestra sobbing, and Maria scolding her in loud and rapid Spanish. Upstairs I heard Ron talking to a screaming Tabbie...I decided to go that direction first. She was lying on the bed, crying and kicking her feet, and Ron was sitting by trying to quiet her. To my surprise, she pointed at me and began to sob, "Mama, Mama!" I picked her up and sat down in the rocker with her. She began to quiet and dwindled down into hiccupping sobs. "Mama," she said again, then stuck her thumb in her mouth and closed her eyes.

"Yes, Gail came back," I said. Oh dear, will Ron resent that she called me Mama? "Ron, she spoke!"

"Not only spoke, but has been screaming 'Mama' all afternoon. Evidently, she has chosen you to be her mama, and you must obtain her permission to go anywhere. She was really very distressed. She thought Mama had left her. I thought we were going to have to get in the car to find you and bring you home."

"Do you mind, Ron?"

"That my ears will never be the same again? Yes. What else besides that?"

"That she called me 'Mama'. Would it be better if she called me Gail?"

"You object to the term, 'mama'?"

"No, I'm flattered, actually."

"You said 'better'. Better how?"

My fatigue had caught up with me. "Ron," I snapped, "don't be a lawyer with me. Your child is calling me Mama. She wants to, and I like it. Ok? But you are her father, and it might be embarrassing to you someday, if other people hear. And what will her mother's people think?"

"Her mother's people stopped being concerned when they discovered Tabbie was autistic. And as for myself, to use your words, I'd be flattered." He kissed my cheek. "Thank you for coming back. We missed you." he said, and left.

Tabbie had worn herself out, and she was soon asleep. I put her down in her little bed. Closing her door, I noted that a deadbolt had been installed, and, checking, I found that there was one on my door also. I stepped out into the hall and listened to the sounds below. Ron and Maria speaking in Spanish. I closed and locked both Tabbie's and my doors, and changed out of my Sunday dress into shorts and a T-shirt. Too much had happened in the last twenty-four hours. I was asleep as soon as my head hit the pillow.

It was almost dark when I woke. Tabbie and Andy were standing by my bed. I smiled at her. "You're awake, Tabbie." She didn't answer but went to the door and twisted the knob.

"It's locked, so the bad man can't get in again. Come on, Sweetie, let me get my shoes on and we'll go downstairs. I'm sure Andy would appreciate a walk outside."

There was no one in sight downstairs but Maria who was cleaning the kitchen. I was not hungry. She volunteered to feed Tabbie, and I went outside to sit on the patio and watch the sun go down over the ocean. It was a calm and beautiful evening. My thoughts turned to the Señora and her problems, and I prayed that, after a hectic and restricted life, she might find the peace she so much deserved. I thanked God that we had bonded well and so easily in so short a time.

"So you are at last awake, Querida," Ron sat down in the chair next to mine.

"Yes. Both Tabbie and I were overtired. I must have slept for a couple of hours. Did you, also, get some rest?"

"A little."

"You put deadbolt locks on our doors."

"I felt it was necessary."

"I agree."

"I will give you a key."

"And who has the other key?"

"I do, of course."

"Ah. You checked our rooms when we were sleeping."

"How else would I know you were all right?"

I decided to let the subject drop. "Ron, the Señora and I talked."

"And...?"

"I found out some interesting things, such as who my natural father was."

"Who was he?"

"A Chilean air force pilot cadet who had come to the United States for special training. He came into the Señora's life briefly when she was a college student, left, and was not heard from again. Interestingly, he was only half-Hispanic. Had a Chilean mother and an English diplomat father."

"Really? Did she tell you his name?"

"Reed. Roberto Reed."

"Will you ever try to trace him, Querida?"

"Well, I have a plate full right now. Maybe sometimes in the future."

Tabbie came out to join us and for a few minutes she and Andy played in the grass together. Then her father joined them in some rough-and-tumble games before sitting down. She climbed in his lap and seemed content to sit there while we talked.

"The Señora is not happy, is she?"

"No. There are things which are troubling her, but how did you know?"

"I sensed it."

"Her girlhood was not happy. She had an overly strict, unsympathetic father who never forgave her out-of-wedlock pregnancy. Hardly would let her out of the house, no type of freedom until Jorge Fuente decided she would make a good and acceptable wife for an important man like himself, and she was allowed to marry him."

"And the marriage? It has not been happy for her?"

"Mixed. Better than life with her father, however Jorge has always had a problem with being dictatorial and temperamental. And it has steadily become worse. Verbal abuse, and maybe worse."

"Sorry to hear it. I think a great deal of the Señora."

"Ron, there are a couple of things she and I talked about, and I wanted to ask your ideas concerning them. When Tabbie was almost taken, do you remember? She kept saying, 'The man, Daddy, the man!'"

"Yes, I remember."

"Do you think she could have seen the man who killed her mother, and linked the two incidents together?"

"But she was in the house when Cara was killed!"

"Where in the house?"

"In her room, or in the room Cara moved into when she moved out of mine—the room you are using now. That was a sort of playroom for Tabbie."

"Both of which overlook the spot where Cara went over the cliff. If she had been at the window—and she could have heard her mother and been there—she might have seen what happened. That could be why it was such extreme trauma for her. She not only lost a mother, she saw her murdered, and it threw her into an autistic state."

"Oh! I see what you mean! And that means that if the murderer heard that Tabbie is coming out of that emotional state, he might have tried to take her and kill her so she could never tell what she saw!"

"That could be. And it would mean that Tabbie is in real danger, and we must take care and watch her very closely."

"Yes, I want to talk to you about that. Until this matter is settled, you and Tabbie mustn't go to the beach by yourselves. Stay on the grounds, and if you wander around the grounds, Ramón should be with you. I hate that it has to be this way."

"I understand and agree completely."

"She was getting along so well."

"She's going to continue to improve. She just needed to know she has us at her back, that we will protect her. She's a strong little girl."

"Thank you, Querida."

"Another thing. Forgive me for asking, Ron, but was Cara on drugs?"

Again, the pause was too long. "I've often suspected," Ron said. "I'm almost sure she was, but we were estranged after Tabbie was born—we didn't share much of anything—bed or board. I do know that she did away with a lot of money, and I suspect that after I drew the line on that her family gave her money. But I have no way of knowing for certain."

"From the way you describe her, it's a pretty good bet she was. Hopefully all of that was after Tabbie was born. Have you thought that her murder, if it was a murder, may have had something to do with drugs?"

"No, I hadn't. In fact, I didn't think. Tried not to think. Just reacted. Your fresh point-of-view may be helpful, Querida. We will throw that in the pot, so to speak. By the way, you are no longer under suspicion. It didn't take them long to check you out. That squeaky-clean reputation was a help."

"Thank God!"

"But..."

"Oh, oh. I was afraid of a 'but'."

"Loro came over while they were here."

I groaned. "Her mother was afraid she might."

"And the resemblance was duly noted. Considered interesting."

"So what do you think they might do?"

"Check out the Fuentes."

"Ron, if they find out about my birth, will they make that fact known? Will Jorge have to know?"

"Just pray not, Querida. I imagine it will depend on how pertinent that fact is to this case. Querida, let's go in the house. I want to put Tabbie down. She's been asleep for some time." Inside I reached for her to take her to her bed, but Ron lay her down on the sofa in the living room, sat down next to her, and patted the seat beside him. "Sit down, Querida, I want to talk to you." I sat. He put an arm around me, drew me to him and kissed me. "It occurs to me that I've been neglecting something important."

I began to shake inside. "And that is...?"

"I want you to marry me."

"Marry you?" I said idiotically.

"Marry me."

I bit my lip and stared at the floor, drew back and looked him in the face. Shook my head, lowered my eyes again to the floor. "Ron, I can't marry you."

A long moment he digested my answer. Then, "Have I made a mistake, here Querida? I thought you said you were in love with me."

"I did. I am in love with you. But I can't marry you."

"And I love you. So what's the problem?"

I shook my head and began to cry. "I can't tell you, Ron."

"You can't tell me?"

"No."

He took his arm from around me and leaned forward to look in my face, raised my chin with his finger. "Gail, what is wrong? I think we are eminently suited for each other."

"We are."

"Then what...? Are you playing with me, Gail? Is this all a big pretense on your part?"

I shook my head again. "No, no, no."

"Are you trying to break my heart?"

"No." Again, I shook my head.

"If we were to lose you, Gail, it would not break only my heart. How about Tabbie?"

"How about you? How about Tabbie? How about <u>me</u>! Have you thought what it would do to me! You reminded me once that you are not sixteen. Well, I am not sixteen either. You are the only man I've ever been in love with in my life. Do you think this is easy? You think I'm playing? I've agonized over it for days."

"Then what...why?"

"I just can't tell you, Ron." I reached in my pocket for a Kleenex. There wasn't one. Ron went to the kitchen, retrieved a paper towel, and brought it back to me. "I don't understand you, Querida. Please tell me."

"I can't."

"Is it that your relatives back in Alabama would object?"

"Get past the 'poor little Latino' thing. They are not like that. And you are not a poor little Latino. You are one of the most brilliant men I know, and I don't care if you are brown, black, yellow or green. That makes no difference to me. You are you, and I love you."

He took my wrists and shook me. "Than please tell me why."

"I can't."

He waited a long moment, still holding my wrists, staring at me, his eyes like those black marbles, again. Then he dropped his hands, which I noticed were trembling. "Gail, I'll call Ramón to come to the house and stay until I return. I've got to get some fresh air, or I'm going to blow."

He left, heading toward the back of the house, and I turned, picked up the sleeping child and climbed the stairs to our rooms, put her to bed. Climbed into my own bed, and cried myself to sleep.

CHAPTER VIII

I felt I had barely closed my eyes when the knock on the door startled me into a heart-pounding wakefulness. I looked at the clock by my bed. It read 3:30.

"Who is it?"

"Ron." I grabbed my robe and opened the door. He was standing there smiling, a light on his face, and joy in his eyes. He was dressed as he had been hours before, but his trousers were wrinkled, the cuffs wet, the shoes wet and sandy. "Can I talk to you, Querida?"

"Yes. I turned on the light. He sat down in a chair in my room, and I sat in a chair facing him.

"I just came to tell you, Miss Templeton, that I am going to marry you."

"Ron...I...."

"No, don't say anything. I have been told by a higher authority that I am going to marry you."

"Higher authority? Who? You have been talking to the Señora?"

"Ah ha! So it's the Señora then who can tell me what this is about! Well, well!"

"I will call her tomorrow." Let her sleep tonight. Tonight I am telling you. No, I don't know what is bothering you, why you are hesitating. But I said I've been talking to a higher authority. I mean God, Querida. I've been talking to God."

"You have?" Had he been drinking?

"Yes. It was a wonderful conversation. He told me that I am going to marry you. Start planning our wedding, Querida! I'll go for any kind, from a Las Vegas quickie to a three-hour church, lavish and expensive. Write your Alabama relatives. Start making up lists. Would you like to meet my relatives? All Latinos from the barrio."

"But Ron..."

"No buts, my darling."

"Tell me please. How...what happened. I didn't know that you even believed in God."

"Querida, I don't know what formula you Born-Agains use to get to God, but my mother always told me He is someone I can turn to when I'm in trouble. And this was big trouble for me. I spent an hour or two walking on the beach, telling Him how much He had betrayed me, how angry I was at Him. Putting a variety of curses into the mix—in both Spanish and English. Then I found myself at that spot where we first looked for anemones. I sat down on the rock you had sat on with Tabbie, looked at that vast sky, and that vast ocean, and knew that He is in control of it all, and that all would be right.

"You're all mine, Beloved."

In spite of myself, and maybe because I wanted so much to, I began to believe in him. "Oh, Ron!"

"Why are you wasting tears, Querida? It's not a time to be sad. It's a time for celebration!" He rose, pulled me to my feet, and took me in his arms.

"You're absolutely mad. But don't stop this diatribe. I love it!" I whispered.

"I am the happiest man alive!" he said, nuzzling my hair. I clung to him like a drowning woman. "Silly, silly Querida," he said. "Don't you know that God made you especially for me? He planned it all a long time ago. He called you to me from a couple of thousand miles away!" He brushed the tears from my cheeks with his fingers.

"God did?"

"God. Yes, He comes well-recommended." He squeezed me in a bear-hug. "Wow, that bed of yours is tempting, but Querida, I don't want a handout. I don't want a drive-up window. I want the whole enchilada. I want a banquet! I want to build a life with you, dream dreams with you, and make our plans together."

"Are we going to have some more children?" I asked dreamily.

"As many as you'd like."

"I'd love to have another little girl with black curls like Tabbie's."

"And turquoise eyes like her mother's."

"And a little boy with eyes which turn into black marbles when he's angry."

"Or however God wants to arrange it. Dark eyes, blond hair. Bue eyes, dark hair. Blonde hair, blue eyes. There are infinite possibilities. And my dear mother, if she were alive, would be impressed. They will be Hispanic."

"With just a bit of English diplomat."

"Well, yes."

"Long live Mothers," I said. "The Señora will be pleased."

"Yes. When I talk to her tomorrow and she tells me why you almost drove me mad by refusing me."

"I love you, Querido."

It was most unlikely--no moonlight, no balcony, no beautiful Juliet and handsome Romeo. Just me, clutching my robe, my feet bare, my eyes swollen from weeping, and Ron, sandy and wet and beside himself with joy. But it was a great love scene.

The next morning I rose early and went downstairs for coffee. Ron was nowhere to be seen. "He go over to see Señora," Maria said. "Have coffee over there. He in very good mood. You sleep with Mr. Ron?"

"Maria!"

"Ok, ok. You gonna marry him?"

"Why are you asking?

"Oh he seem so...like that, you know. He get happier and happier since you come. You think I don't know you in love? He's in love? He stand at window and watch you when you play outside with Tabbie. When he come home from office, 'Where's Miss Templeton?' and 'Does she get many phone calls from men? Do they come to see her?' Speaking in Spanish so you won't know. See him watch you when you not looking, at dinnertime."

"Should I marry him, Maria?"

"Yes. It would be a good thing."

"For him or for me?"

"For both. You can't find no better man."

"Ok. I'll take it under advisement."

"You not open like Mr. Ron. You hide things. But you in love with him."

"Thank you for your advice, Maria." I thought a few minutes. "Maria, I heard Sequestra crying yesterday, and you were scolding her. I hope the child is not in trouble."

"Yes, she's in trouble. Big trouble. With her father and her mother, that one. Sneaking out at night to see that bad boy who also waits for her after school and takes her God-knows-where. She's too young for men. She's not evem had her Quinceanara yet."

"Oh dear."

"Her father takes a strap to her backside. I tell her to come home after school. She is supposed to be here working with me to get dinner ready. No, she's out running with that boy. Leave all work to me."

"That is a problem, but essentially she is a good and dutiful daughter. She'll straighten up. Teen agers have to learn."

"She wants attention from boys."

"Sounds normal enough."

"She's too young..."

"Ok. If I can help by talking to her, let me know."

At that point Ron came in. He smiled at me, cupped my chin in his hand. "The Señora sends greetings, congratulations, and best wishes." He kissed me on the lips, and then gathered me in his arms and gave me another, longer, more leisurely kiss. "Maria, did you know that I am going to marry this beautiful woman?"

"Ah, so you get some sense!" Maria said, coming around the table where she had been working and hugging us both. "I am the first to know?"

"Why not? Who better to be first?"

"Why you take so long?"

"It's not my fault. I think I would have married her after our first really good quarrel. I like the way her eyes flash when she's mad."

Tabbie appeared with Andy at the door to the kitchen, rubbing the sleep from her eyes. I picked her up to hug her, and her father came over to hug us both, give us both kisses, then left for his office.

The phone rang and it was the Señora. "Oh, Señora, did he...?"

"*¡No problema!* I had the pleasure of telling him the salvation story, and he laughed, and gladly accepted the Lord. He said, 'I get Gail along with heaven! I would be a fool not to accept!' My blessings and best wishes, Hija."

"Oh thank you. Thank you so much, Madre. My everlasting gratitude."

"I told you he is a smart man."

"Our Ron is not dumb. Already he talks to God. And, interestingly, God talks to him. Many Christians have never heard the voice of God."

"God's ways are past knowing. *¡Gloria a Dios!* This is the work of God, Hija! I think, if you had accepted Ron without putting God first, He would not have worked so quickly on your behalf."

"True!" My relief was enormous. The Señora had confirmed what Ron already knew, and what I wanted desperately to believe. "Thank you, thank you, thank you, Lord," I murmured over and over again as I hung up the phone. Maria was feeding Tabbie, so I went into the dining room to prepare Tabbie's lessons for the day and collect my scattered wits. So it was really, really true! Ron and I were in love and could plan our wedding! I was stunned, deliriously happy, and terribly frightened, all at once. How could I give Tabbie lessons when I could not concentrate on anything myself? I would have to keep Tabbie inside, since she was in danger, and my troubled four-year-old would have a hissy fit when she found out we could no longer go to the beach or wander freely around the grounds; she was a lover of the out-of-doors.

I was pacing the floor and all of this was going over and over in my mind, when I heard the doorbell ring. It was Detective Milo, talking on his cell phone. I gestured him inside and led him to a small breakfast room off the living room, where we seated ourselves. He hung up, apologizing for the phone call.

"I hoped I would find you in."

"And why is that, Detective?"

"There are some things I would like to go over with you."

"All right. Can I get you some coffee?"

"That would be great." I retreated to the kitchen, poured a couple of cups and asked Maria to keep an eye on Tabbie until the detective left.

"We're just puzzled about a few things, Miss Templeton," he said.

"And those things are?"

"You made a phone call to Mrs. Fuente next door yesterday, asked her not to let Loro come over while we, the police, were here. Why did you do that?"

I stared at him. Oh, Stupid, Stupid, Stupid! Of course, the police would tap the telephone after an attempted kidnapping. Where was my head? I shrugged. "Loro and I look a great deal alike. It often causes confusion."

"I see." He just looked at me. I noticed that he had narrow hunter's eyes, like Ron's. I liked that, and in spite of myself, I began to like Detective Milo. I was determined not to break the silence, however, so I just looked back at him and waited.

"You went to church with Mrs. Fuente yesterday, and to lunch afterwards," he said finally.

"Yes."

"Are you close friends?"

"Very close."

"How much do you know about Mr. Fuente?"

"Very little. I have met the gentleman once."

"Miss Templeton, I believe congratulations are in order."

I groaned. "You have that phone tapped."

"Yes."

"Thank you for the congratulations. Yes, Ron and I are going to marry."

"But it puzzles me why Ron Casabon would have to ask Mrs. Fuente's permission to marry you."

"He didn't...doesn't..."

"There was some kind of stipulation, wasn't there?"

"I am a Christian, Detective. I did not want to marry outside my faith."

"So he accepted that stipulation?"

"Yes. The Señora spelled out the terms, and he accepted them"

"Accepted Christianity."

"Yes."

"Interesting that you would make that stipulation since Ron Casabon would be considered quite a catch."

"That we would agree on. My faith means something to me, Detective. If I had to do without Ron, it would almost kill me. If I had to do without the Lord it would destroy me."

"I have to say, Miss Templeton, after dealing with thieves and thugs, killers, pimps and prostitutes in my profession, it is refreshing to run into a different kind of problem."

"I hope we are not a problem."

"Not a problem. Maybe, a puzzle. Detective work is solving a mystery, deciphering a code, putting together a puzzle."

"Detective, can I ask <u>you</u> a question?"

"Sure. Fire away."

"Do you think the attempted kidnapping of Tabbie has anything to do with Cara Casabon's murder—if it was a murder?"

"That is what we are wondering—one course we are pursuing. We have yet to find a link, but..." he shrugged.

"Detective Milo, when I got Tabbie away from the intruder, and he ran—her father pursued him as far as he could, then returned to her room. She was hysterical, crying. She had not spoken since her mother's death, but she reached out to her father and she spoke. She said, 'Daddy, the man,' over and over."

He nodded.

"Could she have seen that murder and the intruder, and his threat brought back the incident? Could he be afraid that someday she can identify him? Could that be the reason he tried to kidnap her—to kill her?"

He squinted his eyes and frowned. "It does provide motivation, but she is so young. How old?"

"She'll be five this summer."

"And that happened summer before last. There's a possibility there. You said she had not spoken?"

"They had diagnosed her as autistic when I came. But somehow I didn't think it was autism. I think it was neglect and shock. Cara was no mother, from what I hear, and Ron had troubles of his own. He simply checked out, spent his time at his office or at his ranch. Then, if she witnessed Cara's murder, the shock was too much. She just went into a cave inside herself and would not come out."

"Luckily for the murderer, if she did witness it."

"But she is rapidly improving. When I first met Tabbie, she responded to no stimuli—whether spoken or otherwise. None whatsoever. Now she listens and responds, not always verbally, but by nodding or smiling or shaking her head."

"Is this because of your presence?"

"I am going to take some credit. Tabbie badly needed a mommy. She has one now. And fortunately my field is working with exceptional children, particularly preschoolers, so that helps."

He began to write in a little book. "Things to check out," he said. "Where was Tabbie when it happened?"

"Her room. Or my room, which is next door to hers and which she used as a playroom at the time. The windows overlook the cliffs where it happened. If she was looking out of the window at the time..."

"And a little girl needing a mommy might be looking out of the window if she had seen or heard her mama riding in that direction."

"Or saw or heard her mother cry out or arguing with another person."

"Can I see the rooms again?"

"Certainly."

We sent up the stairs to Tabbie's and my rooms. He looked things over carefully again, and then went to stand by the window."

"When I first came here, Tabbie would spend a lot of time at that window just looking out. She doesn't do it as often anymore."

"Having found a mommy." He smiled at me.

"Having found a mommy."

We went back downstairs and to the breakfast nook again. "If your hypothesis is correct, Miss Templeton, it means she is in real danger."

"Ron and I have discussed that. He's given orders that she and I are not to leave the grounds. And if we wander around the grounds, we are to take Ramón with us—Maria's son."

"How old is Ramón?"

"He's eighteen. But he's very responsible."

"Ok. Have Ramón carry a rifle. Not that it may stop anyone, but it may slow them down."

"All right."

"And I noticed deadbolts on your and Tabbie's doors. Who has the keys?"

"Ron and I."

"Carry them on your person. Don't leave them in the house."

"You don't think anyone who lives here..."

"There was no sign of a break in, Miss Templeton."

"Then it is someone...."

"Someone who has access in some way--workman, salesman, neighbor, family member. Or someone passing as a workman or salesman. Any workmen or salesmen in the house in the past few weeks?"

"Not to my knowledge. But Ron or Maria would know more about that."

"Ok, Miss Templeton. You've been a help."

"I have another question."

"Ok."

"Was Cara on drugs?"

He gave me a curious look. "Why do you ask that?"

"I was a psychology major, remember. The way she has been described to me sounds as though she's a classic case of drug addiction."

"You've asked Mr. Casabon this question?"

"He said he didn't know for sure, but often suspected."

"Did she run through a lot of money?"

"A lot. But before her death he had cut her off."

"How long before?"

"I don't remember if he said. A year? Maybe two? He had put her on an allowance she couldn't go over."

"Hmmm. She couldn't have been happy about that. Did a lot of family conflict follow that decision?"

"From what I hear the marriage had conflict from the very beginning, but if it escalated after that, I just don't know.

"Why don't you try to find out some of these things for us, Miss Templeton?"

"About conflict between Cara and Ron? I don't think so."

"Not necessarily. How well do you know Loro?"

"Not well at all. Loro doesn't like me."

"Oh? Why is that?"

"She's been in love with Ron since she was in grade school."

"A pity." He shook his head.

"Why 'a pity'"?

"Well, for one thing, she is due for a big disappointment. She's not going to get Mr. Casabon."

"And the other?"

"Loro might hold the key to knowing more about Cara."

"Why do you say that?"

"Well, Miss Templeton, we have a drug problem here on the Coast. Actually two drug problems. We have the drug problem among the down-and-outers—the street people. And we have the up-and-outers in Cara's and Loro's social echelon, who are into drugs. Mostly cocaine."

"But Cara was older."

"That doesn't seem to make much difference these days. Young people start using and knowing about drugs in junior high, and they had many of the same friends and acquaintances in this small town. Families of that social strata have often known each other for years. If, and how deeply Cara was into drugs, probably Loro would know. And with her interest in Mr. Casabon, she would want all the information she could get."

"Yes, you're right." I sat down wondering why I had not thought of that. "But I can't inform on our neighbors."

"Not even to find Cara's murderer and Tabbie's kidnaper?"

"But...I can't believe the Fuentes' would have anything to do with that!"

"We hope they do not. But we have to investigate everyone, particularly those who are close to Ron Casabon."

"I will help you any way I can, Detective. But I will not hurt the Señora."

He patted my shoulder. "I understand your feelings. But think about it."

He was preparing to leave. "Oh, one other thing, Detective."

"Yes?"

"I had almost forgotten this. One of the first nights I was here, I had bought Tabbie her puppy, and it woke me in the middle of the night, whining. I got up to see about it, looked out of the window, and there was a man there, just standing in the yard, looking up at Tabbie's window. I stood behind a curtain so he couldn't see me, and he moved over to look up at my window, and then left. It was about two o'clock."

"What direction did he go?"

"Toward the front, the street."

"Between this house and the Fuentes'?"

"Yes."

"Can you tell me anything about him? It wasn't Mr. Casabon or one of his workers?"

"It wasn't Ron."

"How do you know?"

"He didn't walk like Ron. He didn't have Ron's physique. Whether it was any of the other men who work on the place, I don't know."

"Black or white? Tall or short?"

"Hard to tell. I was looking down on him, remember. Probably of medium height and build. A little heavy set. White or Hispanic."

"Young or old."

"Not young. Not old enough to walk like an old man."

"Could it be the same person who tried to take Tabbie?"

"No way. That was a young, wiry man."

"He made some more notes. "Ok, Miss Templeton. Thank you for your help." He started to leave.

"Detective!"

"Yes?"

"You didn't answer my question. I know that an autopsy is required in violent deaths. Was Cara on drugs?"

He hesitated. "Yes, she was. Very much so."

"And you have kept that confidential for some reason. You didn't even inform Ron. Why is that?"

"Mr. Casabon was high on our list of suspects. Unfortunately a spouse or lover is to blame for most domestic murders."

"You say 'was'. Is he no longer?"

"He is not completely off our list, but we're thinking less and less about him. Some of the things you've told us have been helpful. We would like to track down the drug angle. Cara's death may be a part of a bigger problem for us—the drug problem. That's why we'd like your help. You want us to catch him or them, Miss Templeton. You don't want fear hanging over your lives or the life of that child who calls you 'Mommy'."

"No, I don't."

We had come to the front door. He stood for a moment with his hand on the knob. "You know, Miss Templeton, the police have access to adoption records, also."

"Oh!" I shook my head. Another thing which I had not thought about. "I hope you do not hurt a lovely lady's family life."

"So Jorge doesn't know?"

"Jorge, nor Luis, nor Loro."

"Hmmm. Very well. We'll do our best to be discrete. But, Miss Templeton, I very much suspect that family life jumped track a long time ago."

As he started out of the door, he turned and grinned at me. "By the way, Miss Templeton, records offices are not open on Sunday!"

I sighed. "I hate one-upmanship, Detective, particularly when I'm the one one-upped! And I seem to be getting one-upped a lot lately."

Tabbie and I somehow made it through the day, and kept busy so that I had almost forgotten Detective Milo by the time Ron was due home. I waited for him by the patio doors and when I saw him, I flew to him to embrace him. He picked me up and whirled me around in his arms, kissed me soundly, and then picked up Tabbie who had followed me out, tossed her into the air. "Ah, my two beautiful girls," he said, and carrying Tabbie with one arm and the other around me, we entered the house. "So, Querida," he said "are we engaged?"

"Oh yes," I said. "We are definitely engaged. You'll never get out of it now, Casabon."

"Nor will you, Miss Templeton, I got you. Ha!" He leered at me.

Dinner was a joyous occasion, the high point of which was when Tabbie pointed to her father and said, "Daddy," and then to me and said "Mommy."

"You got it kid," Ron said. "So Gail came to California searching for a madre and found a madre. And Tabbie searches for a mommy and finds a mommy."

"And Gail finds a home, a child, a husband. How rich can I get?"

"This is 'for richer or poorer,' Gail. Maybe someday we'll lose our money and move to the barrio. Maybe I'll get sick, or you'll get sick, or Tabbie will suddenly get worse instead of better. Will you still love me?"

"Forever."

"Thank you, Querida. And I will also love you."

"Whatever life brings, we'll have each other, and meet our problems with courage and faith. All the good times and the inevitable bad, I'll be there for you, Ron, and for Tabbie."

"And I for you."

That evening Tabbie again went to sleep on the sofa and Ron and I sat together on the loveseat. He took my arm and pulled me into his lap for some serious smooching.

"Querida, let's get married." he said.

"When should we get married?"

"Like tonight?"

"It's a little late in the day. The courthouse will be closed."

"Soon then. Aren't women supposed to plan these things?"

"Ron, I'll have to notify all of my Alabama relatives or risk getting excommunicated from the family. I didn't tell them anything when I left except that I needed to get away for awhile after my mother's death. And I haven't contacted them since. There were too many things up in the air with no resolution in sight. Now I'll have to communicate and make my peace with them, and alert them to the fact I'm marrying a bean-picker."

"A what?"

"Bean picker. In Alabama Mexican farm workers come through in the summer to pick our beans so we call them..."

"Woman, watch your mouth! You're in danger of a beating. How long will all of this take—alerting the family, etc.?"

"You sound like you're in a hurry."

"Yes, I'm in a hurry. I want to sleep upstairs with you and Tabbie. It's lonely down here by myself."

"And your relatives, Ron?"

"Latinos from the barrio. You want them at your wedding?"

"Yes, indeed."

"Cara would not invite them."

"I'm not Cara. Your people are my people, Ron."

"*Mi casa es su casa, Querida,* literally."

"*Y su Dios es mi Dios. Es mi Dios su Dios?*"

"Yes, and your God is my God. That, also, is in the Bible, isn't it?"

"Ruth's words to Naomi, her mother-in-law. 'Your people are my people, and your God is my God.' Ron, why didn't you tell me you are a believer? It would have saved us both some heartache."

"I didn't know I was a believer. I mean, I never disbelieved. My mother told me that there is a God, and Jesus Christ is His son. It never occurred to me to question that.

I've never aligned myself with any group because of a lot of things I've heard. I've never had a serious disagreement with God until my marriage with Cara turned sour, and then she was killed, and they blamed me. I sort of turned off of the whole subject of religion, until you came into my life. Such happiness! I thought maybe God liked me again, when I began to get interested in you. When you refused me all of those old feelings of resentment and bitterness returned. However, when I took that walk on the beach, and I became aware of the vastness of the sky and the ocean, and the greatness of the Creator who made it all. Something became real for me, I found myself talking to God, and I heard His answers in my heart. He reassured me that I had not lost you, and that He loved both of us. It was spooky. It was wonderful. When I talked to Elfrida she gave me the theology behind it, and well, it all fell into place. Does that make sense, Querida?"

"Wonderful sense, Beloved."

"I've heard it said that God tests us. God wanted you to realize that your loyalty to Him came even before your love for me. He wanted me to know the same thing. God said to me, 'Why are you walking on the beach feeling anger and resentment? You are supposed to love Gail. Why is she crying alone? Go tell her you love her.'"

"So you came and...."

"Told you I loved you."

He kissed me again. (Is it just the romantic Hispanic who can talk God, make love at the same time, and feel no contradiction? If this is so, I recommend it to other nationalities.).

"Oh Ron," I said suddenly, sitting up. "I almost forgot to tell you. Detective Milo came by to talk to me today."

"Ah ha! He waited until I was gone so he could see you alone. Ok. What did he say?"

"They know I am the Señora's daughter."

He groaned.

"But I learned some things too. He confirmed that Cara was into drugs. Big time!"

"So now I learn! It would have helped if I had known that at the time. I could have focused my anger. So who killed her?"

"Well, you know you were first on their list of suspects, but they have mostly lost interest in you. They are looking at a drug connection."

"Praise God! Thank Him for favors large and small. But a drug connection! Elegant, proud Cara, killed because of a drug connection like some punk kid shot down in the streets! Do you remember what Cara means, Gail?"

"Dear, doesn't it?"

"Yes, but also in the sense of being expensive. My Cara, killed by some sleazy drug dealer."

"Does a part of you grieve, Ron?"

"Now, Querida, now I can grieve. I couldn't remember any but the bad times before I fell in love with you. But now I remember...she was beautiful. She bore my child. And I occasionally catch myself grieving for a beautiful dead lady. I never loved her as I do you. But I grieve for a situation which was sad, and a regret for a sad world in which beautiful ladies get themselves killed through foolishness."

I reached out for him. "But Ron, remember our old Alabama saying. 'It takes a lot of manure to make the roses grow.' How beautifully your roses grow, Ron. You are the winner. You have Tabbie and Buenaventura."

"And I have Gail."

"Yes, you have Gail."

"I hate to admit it. But probably I could not appreciate you if I had not gone through those bad times."

"Thank you, Querido. Do you know what else the detective told me? He said of all people, Loro might be the key to discovering who murdered Cara."

"The devil he did! Loro! What could she possibly know?"

I explained to him what Milo had said about Loro and Cara being in the same social strata in a small world. "Elfrida is not up on that part of that world. But Loro is."

"And why didn't I think of that?"

CHAPTER IX

Both Loro and Ramón graduated from high school at the end of that spring semester, Ramón at the head of his class, Loro bringing up the rear. Ron went with him to fit and rent a tuxedo for the prom, and prom night he came over for our inspection, decked out in tuxedo and a big smile.

"Golly how handsome you are, Ramón," I said. "Who are you taking to the prom?"

"Going stag," he said. "I asked Loro, but she said 'no thanks.'"

"Stupid girl," I said. "She doesn't know something good when she sees it," which caused him to smile bigger, and probably feel a lot better.

Ron and I went to hear his valedictorian graduation speech along with Manuel, Maria and all of their family. All four of them, Maria, Manuel, Sequestra and José beamed with pride and carried their chins a bit higher when we left. We knew that Ramón was offered a scholarship to the University of California at Santa Barbara, and we were as proud as his family.

But, of course, it was the coming wedding which assumed priority in Ron's mind, and therefore in mine. I was beginning to learn that the driving aggression and strength, which had made him a successful lawyer, would also appear in our private life. An engagement period is something that a woman glories in. She has yet little responsibility, and she can just enjoy being loved. However, for a man it evidently is different, particularly a man like Ron. He was impatient to get to it and get past it. He wanted me in his life, and being a lawyer he would see to every detail to make it happen.

Moreover, I am a confirmed dawdler and dreamer. I wanted to take it more slowly, and I was biting my tongue and asking the Lord for patience in our often clashes.

Our evenings began to be spent filling in the unknowns in our relationship. I began to learn about Ron's extended family as we counted wedding guests. How many siblings? Parents dead, but a set of grandparents who were raising the younger brothers and sister. Uncles? Aunts? Cousins? We came up with about forty who would receive invitations.

And on my side? Uncle Tom, my mother's brother who had inherited the large family farm where I had spent so many happy summer vacations; his wife, Aunt Nan; cousins, Rosamund (or Rosie), nearest my age and my best friend all through our childhood and into adulthood, her husband, Bill and daughter Gabrielle; her brothers, twins Dwayne and Donald, about five years older than Rosie and I, their wives and children. My father had been an only child and he and his parents were dead.

"So that's what? About twenty, Querida? And we have some people here we must invite—Maria's family, the Fuentes', a few of my employees from the office, a few business acquaintances..."

"So much for the small, simple wedding we wanted." I said. "Maybe we can just elope?"

"Don't tempt me, Babe."

"It all seems to be going so fast, Ron. I feel like I stepped into a swift-moving river when we met and I'm still trying to make it to the shore."

The following Friday I came downstairs to find him dressed in blue jeans, a suede jacket, and the inevitable western hat. "We have to go into town, Querida."

"For what?"

"We have to get our marriage license. I've taken off work today because the courthouse is closed on Saturdays. Put on something besides that T-shirt and faded jeans. I might want to introduce you to someone."

"But Tabbie..."

"Maria will care for Tabbie. Ramón is taking a day out of school to help until Sequestra gets home from her classes. Tabbie has to learn to make it without you from time to time."

I could think of no good reason not to obey him. So my dynamic husband-to-be is going to assume control over my life, I muttered in my head as I ascended the stairs and looked through my sparse closet for something appropriate for getting a marriage license. Nevertheless, I realized Ron was right. There was no good reason to wait, and the quicker we got through the multitudinous tasks, the better.

Downstairs he took control again. "Do you have your uncle's phone number with you, Querida?"

"I know it."

He handed me the phone. "Call him. Tell him you are getting married. It's seven o'clock here. It will be nine o'clock there, an ideal time to call."

"Ok," I meekly took the phone. I really was not ready to talk to my family but, again, I did not know when I would be ready and I could think of no good reason not to call. It was long overdue. "Have you got the cordless? You will have to talk to him, you know"

"Ok."

I dialed and heard my uncle's voice.

"Hello, Uncle!"

"Gail! Where have you been? We've been worried sick."

"California."

"What in the Sam hill are you doing out there?"

"I was looking for me, Uncle"

"Did you find you?"

"Yes, I did."

"Do you like the you that you found?"

"I've decided I do, Uncle. I love me."

"That's good. What are you doing out there?"

"Being a private teacher for the little daughter of a wealthy lawyer. She's been through a lot of trauma."

"Well, all right. You're ok, then?"

"More than ok."

"When are you coming home?"

"It might be awhile. There are some complications."

"What kind of complications? You in jail, Niece?"

"Not yet. No, Uncle, I'm getting married."

"Married! To whom?" We heard him cup his hand over the phone and yell to Aunt Nan. "It's Gail. She's getting married!"

"He's Hispanic, Uncle."

"Really? Speak English?"

"A little. We have other ways of communicating." On the other side of the room, Ron was trying to stifle his laughter, holding the phone away from his face.

"Oh, Niece, this doesn't sound good. What sort of work does he do?"

"He works in a tortilla factory in the winter. Next summer we'll be following the crops. We should make Alabama about the bean season."

"You wouldn't be lying to me, would you, Niece?"

"Why would you think that? I'm learning to make tortillas, Uncle."

"Can't you convert him to corn pones?"

"I'm working on it."

"Seriously, Niece, is this guy a Christian?"

"You betcha, Uncle."

"He's ok then, no matter what his work is."

"Can you come to the wedding?"

"Just tell us where and when."

"Will do. Would you like to speak to him?"

"Sure. Put him on."

"Hi, Uncle. This is Ron."

"What's this I hear, Ron?"

"May I have your niece's hand in marriage?"

"Does that tortilla factory pay enough to support a wife?"

"I have a couple of sidelines I do between crops."

"That will help. What's your sideline?"

"I'm an attorney, Sir."

"No kidding? I thought Gail said you are a Christian."

"I am. They are not really mutually exclusive."

"That's news. What's your other name?"

"Casabon."

"Your English is pretty good. How long have you been in this country, Casabon?"

"My people helped settle California in the 1700's."

"Good enough. My people helped settle this part of the country about the same time. You in love with my niece?"

"Very much Sir."

"You want to marry her? All right. We will give provisional consent, provided you are good to her. Wait a minute; are you that wealthy lawyer she works for?"

"Yes, I'm the one."

"You have a daughter, right? No wife?"

"No, Sir. My wife is dead."

"Well. And you are going to marry Gail."

"Yes, Sir."

"How old is your daughter?"

"Four years old."

"About the same age as my granddaughter. Let us know when, and we'll be there for the wedding. Does Gail want to speak to her aunt?"

And so we had to go through the whole thing again with Aunt Nan. Although I still felt I was in over my head in that swift river of wedding preparations, I felt immensely better after talking to my uncle and aunt. I knew the news would be flying through the family and through the town like wildfire, and this would be the first of many calls, now that they had Ron's number.

"Ron, everyone back there will be calling. We had better leave or we will be tied up all day answering the phone." We left it in poor Maria's hands.

By the time we got to the Santa Barbara courthouse I was more in a mood to tackle tasks connected with getting married. The license was secured with no trouble and Ron took some cordial ribbing and congratulations from some of his lawyer colleagues he introduced me to as we met them in the hallways.

"Where are we going now, Ron?" I asked when we left.

"To a bridal shop. We're going to get you a wedding dress."

"Ron, we haven't even picked a date!"

"We'll pick a date. This is the end of May. How about a June wedding?"

"I'll have to find a preacher. He'll have to have a free date. And there is the reception to consider. Bridesmaids and their dresses. Florists. Can I do all of this by next month? How about my family's travel arrangements, and a place for them to stay when they get here? Caterers? Musicians? How fancy are we going to get, Querido?"

"Hopefully not too."

"We'll still try to keep it simple."

"Querida, I have a hunch the Señora would love to be asked to help. Perhaps with caterers and musicians?

"Oh, that's a wonderful idea. If she manages Fiesta every year, a wedding will probably be a cinch. I'll ask her if we can run over to see her and talk about it tomorrow."

The Bridal Shop presented another problem. "Ron, I specifically forbid you to even think of buying my wedding gown."

"Well, that presents another problem. You have not deposited your last three paychecks. So how are you going to pay?"

"I work for this difficult man who lives in the boondocks and will not loan me a car to go to a bank." I grumbled.

"Of course he will loan you a car. He will even give you a car, or you can have half of his car. Or Ramón can drive you. Or you can sign your checks and give them to me to cash. Or, here's another idea…let me put you on my account. Then I won't have to constantly be asked to write paychecks or write checks to florists, caterers, bridal shops, etc., all of which is time consuming, and I don't need time consuming."

"And sign Gail Templeton? Won't that be confusing?"

"Sign Gail Casabon."

"Oh, but I'm not. Yet."

"We'll do that. Besides, I want to tie you to me every way I know how."

"I may clean out your account and take off for Paraguay with a mariachi band."

"Wouldn't be wise. We have an extradition treaty with Paraguay. I'd have to come and get you, and that wouldn't be pretty..."

At the bank, Ron introduced me as his bride, handily leaving out the "to-be". I signed the card as Gail Casabon, looked long at the signature before I returned it to the bank clerk.

"Congratulations, Mr. and Mr. Casabon," she said.

"Thank you." When we turned away, Ron was smiling broadly, while I was feeling like a naughty little girl. Oh how he loved competition and winning! "How does that sound, Querida?"

"Alarming, but rather lovely."

"Seriously, we will have to spend some money on the wedding, Querida. Use this account. They will be mailing us some blank checks in a day or two. When they come to the house, open them, and use them."

"Ron, I have some money from insurance. And I own the house in Middleville, which brings me rent each month. We may sell it; we'll have to talk it over. I thought I might someday live back there, but probably not. I can't see us ever leaving California."

"Not likely. You do as you like with those things, Gail."

"But I want to share what I have with you."

He put his arm around me to hug me. "I love you, Querida. I think of you as the giver, and me as the taker. You've given me back a life. You've given me back my daughter. You've given me the gift of your faith in God. And you've given me yourself

"Thank you, Querida."

"Give praise to God."

"Gloria a Dios," he said.

The unbelievable happened at the Bridal Shop. I found exactly the right gown at the first shop and we disobeyed all the rules of tradition with Ron's helping me pick it out. I did not object when Ron paid for it. I would give him back the paychecks he had given me, although that would have little meaning now that my name was on his bank account.

Leaving the shop, we turned east toward the mountains. "And where are we going now, Señor Casabon?" I asked, knowing that it would probably be like this the rest of our lives—Ron choosing the place and the route, and not bothering to tell me our destination until I asked. I was learning the pros and cons of Ron.

"I though you might like to see our ranch," He smiled at me.

"Oh! Is it a large ranch?"

"No. Only fifty acres. I picked it up for a song when Cara was giving me a bad time. Found it a great refuge and getaway. Haven't had much time to devote to it, but I have a small but good crew out here to keep it going."

"All Latinos?" I asked.

"Of course."

"Haven't you heard about fair employment practices?"

"Find me some Anglos who will do the drudgery of ranch work..."

"Why, Querido, my uncle made me pay my way to summer vacations on the farm by mucking out stables, canning tomatoes, picking and putting up fruit. My cousins were trained to do such things from the time they could walk, and my uncle made me no exception."

"Querida, if you or your cousins ever need a job, I'll hire you. I'll even let you sleep in the main house instead of the bunk house with the boys."

"Do I get to sleep with the boss?"

"Oh yeah! That will be listed in the job description."

We turned off the highway onto a dirt road, and I saw a small Spanish-style ranch house nestled into a valley between two green hills. There were outbuildings and a barn in the back. "Hand me an application for the job, Amigo!" I exclaimed. "I will make immediate application. This is beautiful!"

"I'm glad you like it."

"I love it! When I get mad at you I can come out here to pout!"

"No way! I have pouting seniority. You'll have to brood at home. When we come out here we'll ride horses up into the hills and swim."

"Swim?"

"Swimming pool in the back. Come on, I'll give you a walk-through."

We got out of the car and were walking toward the house when a heavy-set man came out of the front door walking toward us, smiling, extending a hand, speaking in Spanish. Ron shook his hand, answered in Spanish, and then introduced us. "Carlos, this is my fiancée, Miss Gail Templeton."

"Oh, Fiancée! You are getting married, Boss. Charmed," he said to me. "Charmed." He slapped Ron on the back and shook his hand again, smiling broadly.

Ron answered him in Spanish and took my arm to guide me to the front door. "That's Carlos, my old retainer. Keeps the other men honest."

The house was old. The walls were built of adobe brick and were very thick, to keep out the heat, which, this far from the coast, could become brutal. The floor was tile with a few scattered Indian rugs. The living room was dominated by a huge fireplace, and beyond were French doors to the back. I saw a sparkling blue swimming pool beside a patio. Beyond this was the barn and other outbuildings bordered by fencing.

"Oh, it's lovely."

We strolled back through the house. There were four generous bedrooms, and a small den on the other end.

"I like it, Querido, I like it."

"I don't know how many of your family will be coming out, Querida but we can use the ranch house for some of them. They may enjoy the swimming pool, and one of the men will go along as guide if they want to take a ride up into the hills. And drive them to Buenaventura for the wedding."

"What an absolutely fantastic idea. Thank you, thank you! One worry off my mind. We'll put my cousins, Dwayne and Donald and their families here. They have two children each, three of them are boys, and the little girl is a tomboy. They will love it here. Then that leaves Uncle Tom and Aunt Nan, who can stay with us, and my cousin Rosie and her husband who have a five-year-old daughter. Perfect as a playmate for Tabbie. Ron, it's important that she start socialization—being exposed to other people, particularly children, now that she's begun to heal.

"She's beginning to heal," Ron repeated slowly, "What great words. Thank you God, and thank you Gail, and thank you God for Gail." He gave me a hug. "Speaking of Tabbie, we'd better head home."

On the way home we made another stop in Santa Barbara, and this was at the house where Ron had been raised. His grandparents now lived there, raising three of his younger siblings. We drew up in front of a two-story frame home, painted dark green. The front yard showed evidence of being well worn by children at play. A tire swing hung from a tree. On the porch an elderly woman pushed herself gently in a swing, and an elderly man with a walking cane sat in a rocker beside her. Two boys, about ten and twelve played with little cars in dirt in the front yard, while an older boy sat on the porch, his back propped against a post. It was this boy who saw us first.

"Ron, Ron," he called, vaulting off the porch and running toward us. He was joined by the smaller boys and all three ran to Ron's side of the car and began speaking in Spanish, all at the same time. Ron got out of the car and came around to my side to open the door. The little boys stood back, eyes shining.

"Miguel, Roberto, Ricardo," Ron said, "this is my fiancée, Señorita Gail."

They took a moment to digest this fact and then all three took off to tell the grandparents the news. The elderly couple slowly rose and stood awaiting us. "My grandparents do not speak English, Querida," Ron whispered. "I'll have to introduce you in Spanish." As Ron explained in Spanish, they turned their old eyes on me. I waited as they examined me carefully. "They are a little apprehensive," he said. "They remember Cara."

I smiled at them. "*Amas mi nieto?*" the old lady asked.

"Si, mucho, mucho, I love him." I said, and gave her a big hug.

Her face broke into a smile. She hugged me and began to chatter in Spanish. "She would like for us to come in for a cup of coffee." Ron said.

"Ok. Sounds good." She led us past a small dark, but clean, living room, and into the kitchen where a young woman was putting away dishes.

Ron went to her and put an arm around her shoulders. "Anna, I want you to meet my fiancée, Gail Templeton." She smiled shyly and extended a hand for shaking. I noticed that she did look very much like Ron. "We are going to be married next month, Anna. Gail would like for you to be one of her bridesmaids."

"Oh, <u>me</u>?" She said, her eyes shining, wide with surprise. "Oh, I would love to be bridesmaid for you and Ron!"

"And you are all invited to the wedding. It's to be at Buenaventura."

Much excitement as the children hastened to translate to their grandparents, and everyone turned beaming smiles in my direction. Then the *abuela*—grandmother—gave some directions to Anna, who began to make coffee, and stir up some small pancake-like tortillas. We sat at the well-worn wooden kitchen table, drinking coffee, talking, and eating the little pancakes with butter and salt. The grandparents expressed that my hair was *rubia*—blonde—and I did not speak Spanish, had been raised in Alabama, and yet was Hispanic. Ron said that he would tell them my story sometime. They asked us to come back for a family dinner together, and as we left, I reflected that I had never felt more at ease than I did with those gentle people.

"We'd better get back and see if Maria still has her sanity," Ron said, when we were in the car.

Maria had barely been able to hold to it, between Tabbie and the phone calls from Alabama. Thankfully, Tabbie had not thrown quite such a hissy fit as she did when I went to church with Elfrida, and she expressed joy when she saw us. Maria handed us notes from the Alabama phone calls— all ten of them. It was midnight there when I finally got through returning the calls.

The next morning when Tabbie, Andy, and I came downstairs, Ron was already up. He gave Tabbie and me our customary bear hugs and kisses, and then, saying that he needed to make some phone calls, he released me. I escaped to drink my coffee in my favorite spot, the patio, where I could watch Andy and Tabbie frolic in the yard. Suddenly Luis appeared at my side.

"Señorita Templeton!"

"Oh, Luis, you are a will-o-the-wisp. I didn't hear you coming."

"What is this I hear? You and Ron are going to be married?"

"Yes, it's true."

"Please accept my best wishes, Señorita. Ron is a good man."

"Yes, Luis. Thank you."

"His only fault, as I see it, he works too fast. I wanted to court you myself, and now it is too late." He seated himself in the chair next to me.

"I did so enjoy the time with you at the fiesta. You are a wonderful dancer. I look forward to dancing with you again next fiesta." I said.

"Thank you." He nodded at Tabbie. "She is different now. Much better, no? She continues to improve? This is the little dog which saved her life! It is good that you had him. I think Senior Ron did not want the dog."

I laughed. "That was one of our first arguments. But he thinks differently now. We owe Andy a lot."

"I believe the Señora is expecting you this morning. Señor Ron called to say you would be over. I have an appointment for a new job in Santa Barbara, and I have to leave. I wanted to offer my congratulations before I go."

"Thank you, Luis." He gave his jaunty wave and left.

"Well, and what did Luis want?" Ron asked when he came out with his coffee and sat down.

"To offer congratulations and best wishes."

"Good loser," Ron grinned.

"He said you work too fast, that he wanted to court me himself. Probably malarkey, but it sounded good."

"Do you fancy him, Querida?"

"Oh, he is a doll. I love to watch him dance. And his manners are charming. Is that what you mean by 'fancy him'?"

"Not exactly."

"Do you mean do I fancy myself marrying him? Forget it. I can imagine marrying no one but Ron."

"Thank you, Querida."

"Luis is so different from his father. Does it make you wonder what kind of woman his mother was?"

"Not really. I've not spent a lot of time thinking about Luis."

I recognized the murmur of jealousy beneath his words but decided to ignore it.

"How did she die, Querido?"

He gave me a quizzical look. "I've never heard it discussed."

"How did your parents die, Ron?"

"Automobile accident. In Mexico. My mother was an elementary school teacher. During summer vacations, she often went down to Mexico to volunteer a couple of weeks of teaching. She had been teaching at a small village. My father was driving her back to the states. Their country roads are not made for fast cars. He always drove too fast, and he was not able to negotiate a sharp turn. The car rolled over several times. They were both killed instantly."

"What a tragedy for you and the other children."

"Well, particularly for them. I had the benefit of parents during my childhood. I was through college and halfway through law school when it happened. I believe God provided our grandparents who volunteered to raise my brothers and sister. I was the oldest. My sister, Lupe, was married, has a daughter about the same age as our Tabbie. Then comes Anna, Miguel, Roberto, and Ricardo, whom you met."

"I bet I know who pays the bills."

"Do you mind, Querida?"

"Not at all."

"Cara did. Very much. It was strange to me that with all of her lavish lifestyle, she objected to my sending a very modest amount to my grandparents each month to help with household expenses. One of our most bitter quarrels. Well the house is old and paid for. But there are other things—medical and dental bills, taxes, insurance, food, clothing. I could go on and on."

"Yes, I know about household expenses, and I've heard how expensive children can be."

"And I've promised them that if they stay off narcotics and alcohol, tobacco, and away from gangs, keep up their grades, I'll send them to college."

"Fair enough. I am glad you did, Querido. Do you stop by to see them often?"

"Oh, it averages about once a week, depending on how busy I am at the office."

"What do you do about Christmas? Birthdays?"

"Very little. It's been a long time since I've celebrated Christmas. I ignored the holiday. It brought the loss of my parents and family back to me. So, Cara attended the parties of the social scene, and I locked myself in my office and worked. When someone reminded me of a birthday, I got the child a pre-wrapped gift."

"It doesn't sound like you had much fun, Querido."

"No, I didn't have you, My Love."

"I think it would be nice to plan some fun things with them."

"I would like that very much." He rose, took my hand, drew me to him, and kissed me. "I love you, do you know that?" He kissed me again. "We need to go. The Señora is expecting us."

Loro answered the door, her lovely green eyes flicking back and forth between Ron and me, her expression inscrutable. Ron reached out to give her a brief hug. "Hi, where's your mother?" She gestured toward the family room where the Señora rose to meet us, took our hands in hers, and gave us each a kiss. "I am so happy for you," she said, and kissed us again. We sat down together on the sofa by the fireplace, and she and Loro sat opposite us.

"Well, we've got a lot to do, Señora." Ron began.

"When is the wedding to be?" she asked.

"We want a June wedding, he said.

"Which doesn't give us much time," I added. "June is right around the corner."

"How big a wedding? Who is your caterer?" she asked.

"We thought you could make some suggestions, guide us through, so to speak."

"Oh, I would absolutely love that," she said, smiling happily. Loro looked at the floor and swung her foot. Uh oh, trouble coming, I thought to myself.

"Where are you going to be married?" the Señora asked.

"We'd like a garden wedding, at Buenaventura, at a special place overlooking the ocean," Ron said.

"Where Cara died?" Loro asked.

There was a small, shocked silence. "Cara died on Fuente land," Ron said then, and there was ice in his words.

"No, no." I tried to fill in the icy silence. "Just a place directly behind Buenaventura, which has an especially beautiful view of the ocean, and which means something special to Ron and me."

"Oh," she said, twisting a curl and giving a strange little smile.

"Loro, if you cannot be decent, you can go to your room," the Señora said, looking at us with something like desperation in her eyes.

"What is wrong, Loro?" Ron asked. "Both Gail and I have been through a lot of sorrow in the last few years. Can't you be happy for us?"

"Who is she anyway?" Loro asked. "She blows in here from out of nowhere, and walks away with not only the only man I've ever loved, but with my own mother!"

"Loro," Ron said, "you're still in your teens. You have years ahead of you, and the world is full of fine young men. You haven't met them all by a long shot. You wouldn't want me. I'm too old for you. I'm controlling, and Gail can tell you I have a rotten temper."

"I don't care, I don't care, I don't care," she shouted. "Enough of this sweet and reasonable stuff," she stood up and began to sob.

Her mother arose and started toward her, whether to rebuke or comfort her I'll never know, because at that moment Jorge Fuente appeared in the doorway and the Señora stopped in her tracks. "What's going on here?" he asked.

Ron stood up also. "Probably we came at a bad time," he said.

"Papa, he's going to marry her—that woman!" Loro shouted. "And Mama is going to help them. She's going to help with wedding preparations! And she doesn't care if my heart is breaking!"

"Elfrida, what is going on here?"

"What is going on is that your daughter is being both rude and unreasonable," the Señora said.

"You are marrying Casabon?" Jorge turned to me.

"She's nobody, Papa," she said, before I had a chance to answer. "She's a nobody. Maybe if I had been living in his house, sleeping in his bed, as she has, I could have had him, not her. Oh I've seen you out of our windows in your patio, hugging, kissing, and pretending to love poor Tabbie to lure him on."

"I do love Tabbie," I said inadequately.

"Ha! I'll bet."

"Elfrida, for the sake of our daughter..." Jorge began.

"No!" the Señora almost shouted. "No. No more 'for the sake of Loro'. I am going to help Gail plan her wedding.

That is for me, not for you, Jorge, not for Loro, but for <u>me</u>. Because I want to!"

Jorge turned to her and said something in low, rapid Spanish. The Señora drew herself up and answered clearly in Spanish. It was evident that she was not budging. Jorge gave a couple of parting shots in Spanish, put an arm around Loro, and led her from the room.

"Sit down, Ron," the Señora said, and Ron hesitantly sat down again. "I'm sorry. Loro has always been used to having her way. I'm very much afraid that her father has spoiled her beyond the point of no return."

"I'm sorry. We didn't realize..."

"No, no. It's not your fault." She rubbed a hand across her forehead. "We will finish this discussion later. Perhaps we could go to church again tomorrow. You can see why I really need that comfort. And have lunch again afterward? Gail, or both of you, if you would like to go, Ron?"

"I think Gail should go." Ron said. "But I believe I should stay home tomorrow. Gail and Maria have been doing the job of keeping an eye on Tabbie, all week, and now it's my turn. I do want to start attending church with you, as soon as we know Tabbie is out of danger. Gail, what do you think? You and the Señora could make plans..." he nodded toward the doorway, "without interruption."

"I agree. Pick me up again, and I'll take you to lunch this time."

She agreed and saw us to the door with the grace and aplomb of a granddame, not the victim of an abusive father-daughter team.

CHAPTER X

"Well," Ron said, as we walked home. "I see what you mean. That is a house of horrors for the Señora. And what do you think of your little sister now, Querida?"

"I feel sorry for her. I can understand how she could be in love with you. Maybe we're more alike than is evident at first glance. I don't know what I would do or say if I saw you walk out of the door with another woman. I will pray that she finds that someone else and shares the kind of love we have. I forgive her. I've done no wrong, but I hope she will forgive me."

"Maybe she will. I hope so." He drew me to his side. "Querida," he said after a minute, "I have a hunch that Loro will come to the house tomorrow while you and the Señora are at church. I am going to try to talk to her. I have always been a sort of big brother—in my mind, at least. Maybe I can help her to see where she's off track. Maybe I can make her feel better. And I also want to see if I can get any information about the hunch that Milo had, that she would know about Cara's addiction, or where Cara was getting her narcotics."

"You have my reluctant consent. But make sure that Maria and Sequestra are nearby. And Ron remember—she, also, may be using narcotics. From her behavior today I would say it is likely."

"Will do," he grinned. "You know, Querida, if she'd just shut that mouth of hers, she's enough like you..." I gave him a shove. "Naw," he said laughing. "If I had Loro, it would be Cara all over again. Been there, done that, got the T-shirt to prove it."

"Be quiet, Casabon, before you get in deep trouble.

I went to bed early, but could not get to sleep. So many things on my mind. My wedding dress and all of the dreams it brought with it. I had hung it in the closet and returned to look at it at least a half dozen times. Ron's grandparents, the depths of meaning when the old grandmother had turned her eyes on me and asked if I loved her grandson—so full of a hope she hardly dared feel; the smile on the bank clerk's face as she gave her congratulations and best wishes; Carlos and the ranch; and finally the Señora, with her head held high; Loro bursting into tears. And with it all, Ron there, his hand at my back, his smile in my eyes. I was finally drifting into sleep when suddenly I thought of Luis, "The little dog who saved Tabbie's life," he had said, and suddenly I was wide awake. I had told no one but Ron that it had been Andy who had awakened me that night. I sat up, snapped on my bedside lamp, jumped out of bed, threw on my bathrobe and hurried out of my door, being careful to lock the dead-bolt, and hurried to Ron's room downstairs. He answered my knock in boxer shorts and T-shirt, squinting through sleep.

"Ron, did you tell anyone that it was Andy who first woke me the night Tabbie was almost taken?"

"What?" He tried to shake the sleep out of his eyes. "Andy? I—no, no. I don't believe so. As a mater of fact it is something I had almost forgotten."

"Ron, come into the den, we have to talk," I took his hand, forgetting he was not dressed.

"A moment, please," he said, and turned to his bathrobe hanging on a closet door. In spite of my apprehension and questions, I admired, for a moment his broad shoulders and narrow hips as he reached for the robe.

"Ok," he said, putting it on and joining me. "We are discussing Andy?"

"Ron, remember, Luis was here this morning, early. We were watching Tabbie and Andy play and Luis said, 'Oh, that's the little dog who saved Tabbie's life.' Ron, I've never mentioned to anyone but you that I was awakened by Andy's bark."

"I see what you mean," he said. "Besides you and me, only the intruder would have that information."

"Ron, could it have been Luis?"

"You described the intruder as young, wiry, and agile. Luis would fit that description. Do you think it could have been Luis?"

"Luis is young, certainly agile. I don't know! I don't like to think so."

"Querida, right now your mother's house is one crazy, mixed-up mess. Anything is possible. I suppose we'll have to pass that information on to the police." He thrust his hands into his pockets and stared at the floor. "I can't make a valid judgment. I've never liked the guy."

"I just can't believe he would do that."

"Thinking like a lawyer again, Querida. On his side, there is the possibility that he got that information from someone else. It doesn't necessarily mean he's the intruder."

I doubled my legs under me, cuddled to him, and leaned on his shoulder. "I'm still in that swift river current, Querido. Are we going to get out of this, get married, and live happily ever after?"

"No guarantees. I told you this Latino means trouble for you, Querida."

"Forget it Casabon. You'll not scare me away. Your troubles are my troubles. And we're going to lick this son-of-a-gun."

He bent to kiss the nape of my neck. "That's my girl."

"Ron…"

"Hum?" He was nibbling on my ear.

"Ron, we'd better go to bed."

"Whose? Yours or mine?"

"Ours. I mean, our own. Drat it. You are confusing me. I'll see you in the morning, Querido."

"I'll walk you upstairs."

"Can I trust you?"

"Hum. I don't think so." But he left me at my door. Which was a good thing. I was not feeling very trustworthy myself.

When I stepped into the Señora's car the next morning, I noticed that she looked both worn and tired. But she greeted me with a smile. "I am so glad you are going to church with me, Gail. This has been a rough week for me."

"Ron and I seem to have caused a large part of it. I am sorry."

"No, you just helped bring it to a head. And that may be good."

"Bring what to a head, Señora? Is there a specific problem, or is it just family relationships acting up?"

"Hija, you were in my living room yesterday. What would you say?"

"I would say you have a problem which is ongoing and of long standing."

"You say right, Hija." To my surprise, she began to laugh. "How happy I am that we are not those kind of women who pretend everything is wonderful when it is actually awful."

"We call a spade a spade, Madre."

Interestingly and appropriately, the preacher's sermon was about family. "Wives, submit yourselves to your husbands," He read it as the old Apostle had written it. Oh why did God entrust such words to scripture which inspired ego-starved males, satisfied that they had scriptural ok, to spur their wives to a slavery which as often drove as many women to divorce, degradation, neurosis, insanity, or an early grave, as it did to sainthood.

However, only men were educated, only men were permitted to hold down jobs or engage in public life, and only men assumed responsibility in that society. What would he have written to modern women who share education and opportunity, and often assume more responsibility for the welfare of their families than do their husbands? Can such a modern woman graciously accept second place in her family? Can she count on the modern man not to confuse the scripture-assigned primary role of protector, provider, and teacher with ego-status?

Even the most ambitious woman will admit that in every organization there must be a head who has the final say, and because of men's physical strength and built-in aggression, God has given that role to the husband.

When we read past that "submit" in the Apostle's writing, we find that he has given an even more exacting role to the husband. "Husbands, love your wives, as Christ loved the Church and gave Himself for it." We are not used to being told that we must love someone, and modern definitions of love leave much to be desired. Does taking wife out to lunch on Mother's Day fulfill that requirement? Or providing a living? Or maintaining loyalty and not being tempted into other relationships?

Ron, who had jumped light-years ahead of most Christians when he had talked to God in that walk on the beach had told me he had come to the sudden realization that it was not his accomplishments which God was interested in, so much as who he had become. Love involves *being* as much, or more than, *doing*. According to the thirteenth chapter of First Corinthians, *being* patient, *being* kind, *being* humble, *being* gracious and well-behaved particularly in family relationships, had much to do with love.

We think love or not love as a feeling which arises naturally out of the depths of our being. We are not accustomed to being told we must love someone, to think of love as an act of will. Paul, as well as the Old Testament with its emphasis on loving God as the first and greatest commandment, recognizes this, as well as Jesus who added that usually-ignored verse from Leviticus, "and the second is like unto it. Thou shalt love thy neighbor as thyself." Neighbors, like spouses and children are often not very loveable, but we must, as an act of will, love them anyway. Pity the poor husband who is commanded to *love* his wife. She only has to follow his leadership. He has to love her.

This is a commandment hard to specify or fulfill, but Paul continues, "as Christ loved the church and gave Himself for it." So, poor husbands, you not only must love her, but love her with a sacrificial love; love her to your death, not according to any of the strange new definitions of love, but according to Paul's definition of love, found in I. Corinthians 13—being patient when it is not easy, being kind when it goes against our nature; not 'vaunting oneself' which does away with masculine arrogance (as well as feminine vanity); not being 'puffed up' with pride, not misbehaving with 'unseemly' actions; able to hope all things, bear all things, endure all things. An almost impossible recipe for real love—but because men are bigger and stronger, and are given the responsibility of making the family succeed, Paul gave the admonition to the husband, though by extension, it also applies to wives.

Can we achieve that kind of love? It's almost impossible. However, there is a blessing in the effort, in working toward it. How far short modern marriage falls. And in falling short we cheat ourselves, because we never learn the deeper and harder lessons of love.

Then the minister turned to Proverbs 31 and talked about the characteristics of a virtuous woman. I wondered, as I listened to the familiar words, if anyone had ever thought about the husband of the virtuous woman. He allows her freedom to develop her skills in her chosen fields of endeavor. He is a cheering section for her achievements. He allows her to use her own money in the way she, herself, chooses. He is provider and protector and he allows her to oversee his household without his interference. Not all virtuous women will have the patient, kind, and gentle husband who will help her develop into the icon portrayed in Proverbs. Not all virtuous husbands will have the hardworking, kind, and gentle wives who will allow them to become the leader who "sits among the elders" at the gates of the city. But when the combination is there, it is magic, blessing all who are touched by them.

I was twenty-seven. That was late to marry by the standards of the southern states where I was raised. But I had resisted the high school crowd who went in for early dating and popularity contests, and, encouraged by my parents, concentrated, instead upon scholastic achievement. In college, I dated casually, but fell in love with my chosen field of child psychology. And I had been out of college in the work field only a couple of years when there were the illnesses of first my father, then my mother, which had delayed serious dating while I cared for them.

Of course, I had felt stirrings of pain, and probably jealousy also when I had attended the weddings of friends and family, and as bridesmaid watched my cousins, whom I had been so close to marry, one by one.

I had never forgotten a remark made by my cousin Rosie when her daughter, Gabrielle, had been about two. "When you have once held your child in your arms, your arms feel empty without a child, forever afterward." After my arms had held Tabbie a few times, I knew that to be true. She needed my arms around her. My arms needed to be around her. And I knew she was forever my child as surely as though I had borne her.

When the service was over, the Señora and I remained in our seats until the congregation had filed out and the pastor had greeted everyone at the door. On his way back to his office I stopped him and introduced myself, and asked about his marrying Ron and me, and a date for the wedding. We followed him into his office as he consulted his appointment calendar, and gave me several dates in June to choose from. Another of those bothersome details preceding the wedding was accomplished! The Señora and I would tend to other arrangements, consult with Ron, and come up with a date for both the wedding and the required counseling session preceding the wedding. As he shook our hands before we left, he told the Señora he was happy for her daughter, and neither of us corrected him. I didn't care, and, I believe after all she had been through that week with Jorge and Loro, the Señora no longer cared either.

We went to the same little tearoom where we had gone the previous Sunday. "We'll have to find a new place to eat, Señora, if Ron comes with us one Sunday. This would be too feminine for his taste," I remarked.

"What happiness it was for me to be able to tell him about the Lord! There is no greater joy than to be able to lead another person to Christ!"

"He is a strong man, Señora."

"That's the kind who fall the hardest—both for the Lord, and for the women they love."

"Did he have many questions?"

"His parents apparently laid down a good spiritual foundation for him. From what I hear, they were Christian people. Ron went to church regularly as a child, but got away, as many people do, during his teen years. However, he never rebelled against what he had been taught, as some do. He kept his faith throughout college and law school, which is an accomplishment in itself. And he has had no doubt many temptations practicing law. But I've never heard anything contrary to his excellent reputation for hard work and honesty.

"What did I ever do to deserve him? I was so afraid that he was some temptation with which Satan was trying to snare me. I could not marry a man who does not share my faith. I think a real marriage must be built on faith—in God first, and then faith in each other."

"Yes. When you are both Christian, loyalty is to God first, second to your mate, third to your children and extended family. Such a simple plan, but so many people miss it. Some people put children before their mates, which can be fatal in a marriage. Some put everything before God, so every separate action has to be evaluated and judged by both husband and wife, and usually ends up in a clashing of wills and ideals. When the laws and ideals of God come first, each person works to please God, and will please their mates. A man strives to be a husband who 'loves his wife, and gives his life for her.' What wife would not be pleased with that? Children strive to love and honor their parents, whether they are two years old, or eighty. All things work together for good."

"To those who love the Lord and are the called according to his purposes."

"How I wish I had been able to marry in the faith, had been able to raise Loro in the faith. What a difference it would have made!"

"It's not too late." I took her hand. "Never too late for God."

She took a lace handkerchief from her purse and wiped her eyes. "It seems as though one of us is always tearing up, Hija."

"It does, doesn't it? So much to catch up on! How did you find the Lord, Madre?"

"Some of my women friends began to attend a prayer group in someone's home. Some of them began to be saved. One of those was me."

"How great these groups in homes are. One is not always free to go to church, and sometimes the church program does not fit our needs."

"Yes. I always felt tossed around in a chaotic world before I found the Lord. It's different now. The world is still chaotic, but I've found a measure of peace, even in chaos."

"'The Lord is my refuge and my fortress,'" the Psalmist said.

"Oh yes."

"Señora, tell me about Loro."

"I wish I could. I'm so worried about Loro."

"She's on drugs, isn't she?"

"Oh Hija, I don't know. I very much fear she is. She was before. She has been to rehab, and I thought she would be all right. I did so hope she would be. We were devastated when we discovered she was using narcotics the first time. I have never known Jorge to be so angry. But he doesn't understand that one must handle the drug addiction with tough love, not reward them with spoiling."

I felt a little sick. I had found out more than I wanted to know. But if we share our loved one's joys, we also have to share their burdens. "What can we do to help her, Madre? Can we have an intervention? If she is back on drugs, and judging by what I saw and heard she is, she needs to be back in rehab. And she needs to be away from her father. He is literally going to kill her with love. It's probably a stupid question, but do you think she would consent to be my bridesmaid?"

"You want her to be your bridesmaid after she was so rude to you?"

"She would help tie my past and future together. Rosie, my cousin, will be my matron of honor, and Anna, Ron's little sister will be the other bridesmaid. The past and the future. Loro would represent Buenaventura, and La Fuente, and you, Madre. And while we are on the subject, would you, along with my Uncle, give me away?"

"I would love to. It will be the second time I have done that, will it not, Hija-- Give you to someone I love and trust."

"People will talk, we look so much alike."

"I no longer care, Hija. Jesus said, 'Ye shall know the truth, and the truth will set you free.' I should never have kept it a secret. I will be telling Jorge, and Loro and Luis soon that you are my daughter."

"Thank you. I pay no attention to what Loro did and said yesterday. That wasn't Loro talking. That was the cocaine. If we could get her into rehab soon, she could get sober enough to be my attendant. The fact that she loves Ron is a great compliment to him and to me. I appreciate that fact, and it will always make me love her a little better."

"You are not afraid that she will try..."

"I trust Ron. No, I think we can look back at this together some day and be good friends, Loro and I. If not, then I will accept that. But I still want her to be my bridesmaid."

"If we plan an intervention, I want Ron to be there. And you come, also, I believe she will feel your love for her.

Now, Hija, how many guests are you going to have at your wedding?"

For a while we talked about the wedding. We would prepare for one hundred. The Señora wrote in her little notebook. What would we serve at the reception?

"I would like deep South food and southwestern food."

"Ah," The Señora wrote in her notebook. "Watermelon and fried chicken, fajitas, pintos and Spanish rice. And condiments."

"With cilantro, please. I've developed a taste for it."

"Of course."

"Aunt Nan will insist on making her special potato salad, so we must work that in, somewhere."

"Goes well with Southern fare. Dessert—besides the wedding cake?"

"Nothing but Maria's delicious pan dulces."

"And ice cream cones for the children."

"Oh yes, of course."

"Hija, unusual but fun--blending Latinos and Alabamians. What makes it most wonderful is that you are not attempting to impress anyone but just have a wonderful wedding celebration with the people you love. Tell me about your wedding dress."

"Sweetheart neck, princess style, hip hugging with a gradually full skirt, three flounces. Ankle length because I will be walking on grass. Faintly reminiscent of a Spanish dancer's costume."

"I love it! Veil?"

"Only a small one on a circlet of flowers."

"A morning or evening wedding?"

"Six o'clock in the evening, so we can take advantage of the sun setting over the ocean. That will mean a leisurely drive down from Santa Barbara for Ron's relatives, a leisurely drive from the ranch for some of my relatives who will be staying there, as well as for the ranch hands who will be coming. No getting up at dawn to be here for a ten o'clock wedding. Besides who wants watermelon, fried chicken, and fajitas for an early lunch?"

"You have a point. What will Ron be wearing?"

"I want him to wear something western. I love Ron in his suede coat and starched blue jeans, his inevitable western hat. For those who can wear it, a western hat makes a man terribly handsome and sexy. But we'll want him to be a little dressier than that, of course."

"Maybe I can help with that. What sort of music will you have?"

"Maybe a string combo for the wedding itself. What would you think of a mariachi band for the reception?"

"Lovely. Is Tabbie going to be your flower girl?"

"Yes. And my cousin Rosie's daughter, and Ron's niece, all about the same age."

The señora wrote some more in her notebook.

"I might mention that we will have to have extra security for Tabbie. It would be an ideal time for whoever tried to take her to try again. Ron and I will be busy, and there will be a crowd."

"Very sensible. Have you thought what kind of cake you will want?"

"Traditional, three or four tier, with sheet cake to splice out in case we run out.

"Good. You have pretty definite ideas! We will work together on these things, Hija. You will have a most beautiful wedding. I will contact musicians and caterers and place orders. You will see to the bridesmaids' dresses and flower girls' dresses, and the cake."

"Yes, yes. And thank you for your help. We will keep in touch. Meanwhile about the intervention for Loro..."

"You will help me with that? You have studied such things."

"Yes. Don't say a word to Loro. She's not to know until everything is ready."

"I don't want Jorge to know."

"Do you know where she may be gutting her narcotics, Señora?"

"No, but..." she hesitated a long moment.

"But?"

"A long time ago, before Cara died, before her last rehab, she once said something about Cara which made me suspicious that Cara might have been giving it to her. But then Cara died."

A cold chill crossed my mind and I heard again Ron's words. "Cara was killed on Fuente land."

"And so if she was ever a source, she certainly is not now."

"No."

"There was a silence I looked at the Señora's face—a face which had become very dear to me in a very short time, sad shadows played around her beautiful eyes. I put my hand over hers. "Señora, in the South we have a saying when we encounter problems. We say, 'We're going to lick this sucker'. God has His reasons for everything that happens to those He loves. Now let me tell you some of the exciting things which happened to me when I was a child, you missed out on." Then I proceeded to tell her of all the minor disasters which had befallen me—the time I fell off my uncle's hay wagon when I was five and broke my arm; being out of most of the second grade because I had pneumonia; my first date in high school. I regaled her with the upsets of my childhood right through my senior prom, when the limo was late, it had a flat tire, my date lost my corsage, and I stained my rose-colored dress with green punch.

"No romance previous to Ron?"

"Oh yes. I fell madly in love with my music teacher in junior high school, and I thought briefly I had found my dream man in my senior year of college, but it didn't work out. He was too nice and even-tempered. I would have driven him nuts, and he would have bored me to death. He found a nice and even-tempered young woman in his hometown after we graduated.

The sadness was gone from her eyes and we were sharing laughter again as we drove home. But underneath, I felt the heavy burden of a younger sister caught up in a web of narcotics, and Cara murdered.

I was exhausted when I walked into the door. I put my hat and purse on the living room table (a privilege I had adopted since I had become prospective lady of the house) and listened briefly at the bottom of the stairs to see if I could hear Tabbie. I heard nothing but the murmur of men's voices from the dining room. Ron rose to greet me as I entered and gave me his bear hug and a kiss. Detective Milo rose and extended his hand. "Good to see you again, Miss Templeton." We shook hands and I sat down with them.

"Tabbie ok? " I asked.

"Ok. Upstairs asleep. Sequestra is with her."

"Good. Is that coffee, and can I have some?" Ron called to Maria to fetch me a cup.

"What is Maria doing here? This is her day off."

"Something about Sequestra. I don't think Maria trusts her daughter out of her sight anymore."

"Ah yes. Love is painful when one is fifteen." Maria brought me my coffee and I took a sip gratefully.

"Did you learn anything from your talk with Señora Fuente?" asked the detective.

I took another long sip before I answered. "Gentlemen, I haven't known the Señora very long, but I love her dearly, and I don't want to be used to pry information from her. If you use anything I tell you to hurt her, I'll do something dreadful to you."

"Hey, I love and respect her, too," Ron said.

"Miss Templeton, our ultimate purpose is to help, not hurt. I think the Señora has some very serious problems that need to be addressed. We may be able to help solve them."

"Did you learn if Loro has been using drugs?" Ron asked.

"Yes. She has already spent time in rehab. Elfrida is afraid she is using again. The situation is aggravated by

Jorge, who will not take a strong stand but continues to spoil Loro and give her money."

"Oh boy," Ron said.

"Did she come over while I was gone, Ron?"

"Yes, and it was more or less a repeat of what went on yesterday. However, I did get my big brother lecture in. Not anything she wanted to hear. She was still here when Detective Milo dropped in, and she scuttled home. I did have a chance to tell Milo about Luis' mentioning that Andy had helped save Tabbie's life."

"Yes, that is very interesting," Milo said. "It means that Luis, or someone close to Luis, is our guilty party."

"I learned one other thing from the Señora. She says that Cara might have been supplying Loro with drugs."

"Cara!" Ron exclaimed.

"Whoa! That is interesting," Milo said.

"It was a guess on the Señora's part. She said Loro had mentioned something once that gave her that impression. That was before Loro went to rehab."

"Cara dealing drugs! I can't believe it," Ron said.

"Didn't you say you had cut her budget because she was spending too much money?" I asked.

"Yes, I did. But she didn't stop spending money! I thought she was getting money from her parents, though when I confronted them, told them they weren't helping matters, they swore they were not financing her."

"The next question is, where was Cara getting her cocaine?" I said.

"And that's a big one," Milo said. "That's where narcotics and homicide will have to cooperate."

After Milo left, Sequestra came downstairs with a sleepy Tabbie, who needed lap time with her daddy or mommy. Ron took her, while I took our cups into the kitchen. "Maria, Sequestra just came downstairs with Tabbie. Why don't you go home and get a little rest?"

"Thank you Miss Gail. We'll go. I don't know if you gonna be gone long, and if Mr. Ron is gonna leave. Sequestra lost her key, and I'm not gonna ask Mr. Ron for another one. She stay out late with that boy, and I'm not gonna let her do that. He meet her when she leave here. You know?"

"You're a good and vigilant mother, Maria. And I know being a good parent can be exhausting."

Maria and Sequestra left for their house, and Ron and I took Tabbie and Andy out on the patio to play and enjoy the late afternoon. I had bought Tabbie a small ball that she and Andy could play with, and Ron tossed it to Tabbie while she and Andy fought over it. Andy usually won, and would take victory laps, carrying the ball in wide circles around the yard while Tabbie chased him, yelling "Andy, Andy!"

Ron stopped and looked at me. "She said 'Andy', Querida," he said, and came over to sit down by me and put his head in his hands. Seeing that he was crying I pulled him over to me, hugged him, and put my cheek on his.

"I told you she is healing, Querido. I told you."

"And so she is."

"And I will tell you what I want you to do. When you play together, speak to her in Spanish. She gets English all day from me, and I want her to retain her bilingual ability. I want her to be able to play with the children in your family, and talk to her great-grandmother and father in their own language."

"I do so love you, Querida."

"Gloria a Dios," I said.

Tabbie came to her daddy and climbed on his knee. "Play, play," she said, and he looked at me and smiled, kissed her gently and went back with her to the yard to throw the ball—mostly to Andy. I sat watching them, being thankful for the moments in our lives of pure and simple love and peace, sometimes in the middle of awful chaos. Finally, Andy and Tabbie wore themselves out, and Ron came to sit down by me, take my hand in his, and just hold it. We sat a long time in that perfect peace, Tabbie and Andy rolling in the grass at our feet while the sun eventually began to sink into the ocean.

"Did you ask Maria why she came over?" Ron asked.

"Sequestra. You know she has a boyfriend, and that upsets Maria and her husband. They believe she is too young to date. He has been meeting her after school, and after she gets off work here. Maria doesn't want her meeting him, so she's keeping a tight rein. It looks like when you call Sequestra to come and sit with Tabbie, Maria is going to have to come with her to watch Sequestra."

"The joy of being a teen-ager's parent," Ron grinned.

'It seems that Sequestra has lost the key you gave her to the house, and Maria doesn't trust her with another key or to lock up if you leave."

"Sequestra lost her key?"

"Yes."

It hit us both at once. "That's the way the intruder got into the house that night!" I said.

"Bingo!"

"Let's go inside and call Milo."

However, after talking to Milo we were more confused that reassured. We thought that Sequestra would tell us the name of the boy friend, the police would pick up the boy, and we would have some answers. But since the police had found out that the attempted kidnapping of Tabbie and the murder of Cara were tied up in the sale and distribution of narcotics, it was not that easy. "See if you can get the name of the boy from her," was all he said.

Ron had the house phone, I had the cordless. "Gee, we were hoping..." I said.

"Seems nothing is simple anymore," he said. "Our work is usually in a lot of small details, not one big one. Remember the jigsaw puzzle I told you about, Miss Templeton? We have to fit the pieces. We'd like to catch the bigger fish, the people who are distributing the narcotics, and that is taking time. But this is an important piece of information. Keep digging, and we'll do the same on this end."

We hung up a little discouraged, but we didn't have time to brood. "Eat, eat!" Tabbie said, pulling on my skirt.

"Ok, pudding." We went to the kitchen, and I made some sandwiches, and we found some soft drinks and ice cream.

"You can cook, Querida?"

"What Alabama girl can't cook? But I still have to learn how to make tortillas. Corn pone I can manage."

"I'm a lucky man. Abuelita will teach you how to make tortillas."

"I'm looking forward to it." We took the quart of ice cream out of the freezer and found three spoons to eat it with. "What is your favorite flavor ice cream?" I asked Ron. "Wives need to know things like that."

"Chocolate. Yours?"

"Maybe strawberry or cherry. And Tabbie's?"

"Chocolate!" she said promptly. I held up my hand for Ron to give me a high five, which he did, grinning with joy.

"Just like Daddy.

"Like Daddy." This time it was I who cried. Tabbie was not only saying new words, that little head of hers was computing information. Sometimes the world is just too full of joy. It leaks out in tears.

CHAPTER XI

When Sequestra came in from school that Monday evening, Ron, who had taken off work early, was waiting for her with his grimmest expression—and it wasn't an adaptation for an errant teen-ager. He had talked to Maria and her husband, Manuel, and gotten their permission and backing to have a good heart-to-heart with their daughter.

"You have to be there," he told me.

"And why is that?"

"Thinking like a lawyer again. I'm going to stop just short of throttling this young lady, and I need a witness that will attest to the fact I did not or have not broken any bones or made any sexual overtures should it ever come to trial. Young people know entirely too much about such things these days."

When Sequestra arrived, Maria brought her to us from the kitchen. Ron opened the door to his study and gestured her in, seated himself at his big, walnut desk and began without smiling. "So, Sequestra, you have lost your house key."

"Yes, sir," she said, timidly.

"When?"

"It was the night of Fiesta when I stayed over with Tabbie."

"Ah! The night Tabbie was almost kidnapped! And did you lock up when you left?"

"Yes, sir. I remember I locked the door."

"Are you sure of that?"

"Yes, sir. I remember very well locking the door."

"And after you locked the door what did you do with the key?"

"In the pocket of my jeans, Mr. Ron."

"You remember putting it in your pocket?"

"Oh yes. But when I looked in my pocket for the key it was not there."

"So where could you have lost it, Sequestra? If you went straight home as you were supposed to do?"

"I don't know."

"But you didn't go straight home, did you, Sequestra?"

"But I did, Mr. Ron!"

"No, you didn't. You are lying, Sequestra. There was someone waiting for you at the back door, who saw you lock the door and put the key in your pocket. Someone who had probably met you before and seen you put that key in your pocket."

"Oh no, Mr. Ron, I..."

"Oh yes, Sequestra. Don't keep on lying to me. That is what happened isn't it?"

"But it just happened, Mr. Ron. I didn't mean to lose the key. It just happened. It must have fallen out of my pocket."

"How could it have fallen out? Those blue jeans pockets are pretty deep. Did you sit down and talk with your friend for a while?"

"Just a little while, Mr. Ron. We didn't do bad things. Just talked for a little while."

"But he maybe gave you a kiss or two? You are an attractive young lady. It was a beautiful night. There was music coming from the Fiesta next door. Any young man would have given you a couple of kisses."

"Well, maybe one or two, but we didn't do bad things."

"Oh, I think you did, Sequestra. Because it would have taken more than a couple of kisses to get that key out of your pocket. And that young man took that key out of your pocket."

"No, he didn't do it. It just fell out of my pocket."

"Oh, it was him, all right, Sequestra, and he, or one of his buddies used it to get back in my house and try to kidnap my daughter."

"No! Why would he do that? He doesn't know Tabbie. What would he want with Tabbie? He didn't try to take Tabbie!"

"But he did, Sequestra. Some one wants to kill Tabbie because she was, in all probability, a witness to the murder of her mother. She hasn't been able to speak, but she is regaining her speech, and may be able soon to tell us who did it!"

"No, my friend did not murder Tabbie's mother!"

"I do not think he did. He's too young and stupid to be able to get away with it. But if someone offered him money to kidnap Tabbie, I think he is young and stupid enough to try to pull it off."

"He would not do such things."

"I believe he would. Give me his name, Sequestra."

She shook her head and began to cry. "No, Mr. Ron."

"Yes, Sequestra." Ron's eyes had that fire in them again. "Or would you like to go to jail for helping him in an attempt to kidnap my daughter?"

"No, please, Mr. Ron."

"Sequestra," I said. "You think he loves you, don't you? That's why you are protecting him."

"Yes!"

"If he loves you, why is he making love to you so he can get the key? While he was kissing you, his thoughts were on the key and the money it might bring him. What kind of love is that? While he is enjoying your protection, Mr. Ron is getting ready to call Detective Milo to come and pick you up and take you to police headquarters where they know how to get information out of people. Wouldn't it be better to avoid that by just giving Mr. Ron his name?"

"He does, too, love me!" she said in a small voice.

"I wouldn't count on it," Ron said.

"If this is all a mistake, we will find out. And it will be over," I said. "But it is not going to go away. And frankly, Sequestra, I hate to see you waste your good looks and sweet spirit on someone who would make love to you just to get your key. You can do a lot better than that."

"It's Michael."

"Oh," Ron said, reaching for a note pad. "Michael who?"

"Michael Garza. He works for Mr. Fuente."

"Right next door! Convenient," Ron said. "He's got family who lives on the place?"

"No. Just him. He's got a room in the stables and helps with the horses."

"I see. Thank you Sequestra."

"I didn't mean to...I didn't know, Mr. Ron. I didn't know about that being the key the intruder used. I just...I'm sorry."

"Sequestra, what Gail said is right. You can do a lot better than some jerk who takes advantage of you to steal something you have. You're way too young to be getting involved in such things as serious petting, which we both know you were doing. I don't want to hear about any more of this kind of conduct. You obey the rules your mother and father lay down for you. Stay away from this boy and others like him. They're bad news, understand?"

"Yes, sir."

"You're free to go."

"Thank you, Mr. Ron."

When she left Ron still sat at his desk and staring into space. "Querida, I don't like the way all of this keeps leading back to La Fuente."

"I remember when you said, 'Cara was killed on Fuente land,' Ron. I knew that, but it put a chill down my spine."

"And I remember when you said, 'We're going to lick this sucker.' I had somewhat given up at that point. Cara had been dead for over a year, and we didn't seem any closer to knowing who or why or even if she had been killed or if it was an accident. That gave me incentive to keep going. Sit down a minute, Gail. I want to call Detective Milo and give him this information."

He made the call and hung up. I started to rise. "Sit down," he said. "I want to show you something."

. He opened his safe and took out a very old and frayed ring box. Inside were two antique wedding rings of Mexican design, filigreed with heavy gold leaves encircling them.

"Lovely!" I put the smallest one on the ring finger of my left hand. It fit.

He put the other one on his own left hand. "Both of them look like perfect fits. They belonged to my parents, Querida, and to my father's parents."

I placed my hand over his. "Then these are a wedding gift from your mother and father? Oh, Ron, shall we use them for our own?"

"Would you like that?"

"Did Cara...?"

"They weren't Cara's style, Querida. I had enough sense even then to know that."

"I'm sure she was a woman of style, Ron, but not your style. I'm surprised that neither of you recognized that."

He shrugged. "Water under the bridge."

"But I forgive you, because you made a beautiful baby, who now belongs to me."

He grinned. "Wanna make some more?"

"All in good time, Querido. But back to the rings, I love them"

"And what sort of engagement ring would you like?"

"What sort did you have in mind?"

"Knowing you, Querida, I haven't made a purchase or even thought about it too much. I had a hunch you would have some original ideas. And picking out something which would go well with my grandparent's wedding rings is beyond me, anyway."

"Do we have to have a diamond?"

"Wouldn't you like a diamond?"

"Diamonds are beautiful, but I always thought they were a poor symbol of love. Too hard and cold."

"What is your birthstone?"

"Opal."

"Ah, Querida! I maybe know just the thing. A fire opal! Hard to find in the states, but plentiful in Mexico, because they are mined there. Let me get you a fire opal. They are very colorful and bright, more so than a regular opal. Would you like something like that?"

"It sounds lovely. But it will probably have to be custom made to compliment the wedding band."

"Ok. We'll work together on the engagement ring."

Later, just before the dinner hour, the phone rang and it was the Señora. "Could you and Ron come over?" she asked. "I need you."

"What is wrong, Señora?"

"I told Jorge and Loro about us. That I am your natural mother. They both went a little wild. I'm frightened."

"My presence will not aggravate the situation?"

"Maybe, but I don't care. I need you and Ron, now."

"Luis is not there?"

"Luis has a new job in Santa Barbara, and is staying in the condo there."

"We'll be right over."

La Fuente never seemed colder or more forbidding. The Señora met us at the door and flung herself into Ron's arms. "I am so frightened, Hijo," Ron and I put our arms around her. "I don't think Jorge is quite sane."

Ron stepped back to look at her in the dim light. Her face was puffy and scratched. "How long has he been abusing you, Señora?"

"It wasn't so bad until a couple of years ago."

"He didn't take the news of Gail's relationship well?"

"No. That's putting it mildly." She led us into the drawing room where Loro sat in an easy chair, her feet tucked under her, her eyes very big. Ron acknowledged her with a nod as she followed him with those big eyes across the room where we sat down.

"Where is Jorge now?" asked Ron.

"I don't know. Maybe he's in his room; maybe went out to walk. I should tell you, he is drinking, and that makes him act worse."

"Loro, do you have any wine in the house?"

"Yes."

"Get a glass of wine for your mother." To my surprise, Loro left with no argument and returned in a moment with a small glass of wine. Ron took it from Loro and handed it to Elfrida. "Drink it, Señora."

"Have you watched your father abuse your mother often?" Ron asked Loro.

"No. Not...I mean I wasn't home most of the times it happened. I..."

"Why didn't you call the police when it happened, Loro? Spousal abuse is against the law."

"Is she..." she looked at me. "Are you really my sister?"

"I am."

"Who is your father?"

"My natural father? I understand he was a Chilean air cadet, the son of a British diplomat. But why don't you ask your mother about him?"

"Why did you come here?"

"To find the Señora, my natural mother. I was raised by wonderful parents in Alabama, but they both died during these last two years. I ran across my original birth certificate, found Elfrida's name and, on impulse, came to California to find her. But I lost my nerve and was sitting on the beach when Ron found me. He spoke to me because he thought I was you."

"Is that the reason Mama loves you and doesn't love me? Because you are the daughter of the man she never stopped loving?"

"Her love for my father or your father has nothing to do with the love she feels for you and me. I happen to know she loves you dearly."

"Sometimes you are pretty unlovable, Loro," Ron said. "But your mother will always love you, whether you are loveable or not. She's that kind of lady."

A door slammed in the back of the house. We heard footsteps, and Jorge came to the door of the parlor and spotted me.

"Ah, There is the wretched woman who has destroyed my family!"

"Jorge, if you don't want your block knocked off, don't say anything else," Ron said. "You are evidently used to winning your arguments with Elfrida, judging from the marks on her face. But I'll be a little harder to handle."

"Ah yes, the mother," Jorge said, ignoring him and glaring at Elfrida.

Ron rose, took off his coat, made an elaborate ritual of folding it carefully, put it on the back of the chair, stepped back, and backhanded Jorge across the face. Jorge stumbled backward, his glasses flew across the room. "Sit down, Jorge," Ron said. "Loro, please get your father's glasses for him"

"Call the police, Loro," her father said.

"Ask for Lieutenant Milo," Ron said. "He'll be interested to learn your father is a wife beater. He's already interested in the fact Cara was killed on Fuente land, Loro has been in rehab and needs to go again, and my house was invaded, my little daughter almost kidnapped by a Fuente employee."

Jorge sat down abruptly. Loro, who had risen, also sat down. They both stared at Ron.

"Señora," Ron said, "what do you want to do? Do you want to have this man incarcerated?"

"No, no," Elfrida said. "Please, no."

"But you are afraid to stay here."

She nodded without speaking.

Ron looked at me. I knew he was asking if Elfrida could stay with us at Buenaventura. I nodded. "Ok," he said. "But you are going to report this to the police so they will have a record of it." He took out his cell phone, dialed a number, and gave it to Elfrida. "Just tell them to send an officer out to take the report."

Looking very frightened, but not taking her eyes off Ron, she did so, and handed the phone back to him.

In a remarkably short time, the police arrived and took their reports, including a picture of the Señora's battered face. When they left, Jorge confronted Elfrida. "Well, are you satisfied, Elfrida? I'm a ruined man."

"The only one who has ruined you, is you," Ron said. "Don't blame us. We've just taken the wraps off of your actions."

"Señora, would you like to spend a couple of days at Buenaventura until you can get things sorted out?" I asked.

"I would like that," she said, and left to pack an overnight bag.

"Loro?" I asked.

"I will stay here with Daddy," she said.

The Señora's temporary move to Buenaventura was a smooth one. I put her in the upstairs room next to mine. The first day she kept to her room and cried, but the next day she came downstairs, and volunteered to watch Tabbie play outside while Maria and I conferred about lunch. Tabbie, who had already met her a few times, took to her immediately and enlarged her world to include a grandmother. That was good because there is nothing like a child to get, and keep, one's mind off one's own problems. The next thing we knew, she had the Señora by the hand and was leading her around the patio, pointing out to her the flowers and shrubs. She still did not name them, but would point at them, and wait for a reaction, and of course, the Señora would react.

Aside from Tabbie, we were about to be thrown into a flurry of wedding activity and here the Señora's help was invaluable. We had to decide on the wedding party. Ron called his sister Lupe, whom I had not yet met, to ask if her little daughter would be flower girl along with Tabbie and Gabrielle (whoever heard of three little flower girls? But that was the way I wanted it—to display Tabbie and two other beautiful little girls in the family was just too tempting!). Lupe was thrilled. She said she would not send the measurements for Letitia's little dress, but would come herself to meet us and help with anything she could.

The very next day I received a call from Rosie in Alabama, saying that she and Gabrielle, her daughter, would arrive early in order to help with wedding preparations, and be able to visit before the rest of our family arrived.

Rosie and Gabrielle arrived at the Los Angeles airport a couple of days later, and Ramón, who was a better driver in heavy traffic than I was, drove the Señora and me down to meet her. I hadn't known I had missed my Alabama family so much! My California life had been so full and busy, but I found myself tearing up and my hands becoming sweaty with impatience and the anticipation of seeing her again. When she came toward me with Gabrielle in tow, we hugged for a long moment and there were tears in both of our eyes.

Then I picked up Gabrielle for a hug and introduced them to the Señora.

Her keen eyes looked my cousin over. Rosie is one of those angular women who wear suits and slacks well, even though she is not much taller than I am. Her dark hair is straight and silky, and no matter what she wears, she looks sleek and tailored. She looked extremely sleek and tailored in a linen dress and high heels. She could always dance around in high heels—which I was never able to do. And Rosie looked at the Señora, her immaculate grooming, her turquoise eyes, and her lovely smile. "So you are Gail's natural mother!" she said. "I can see where she gets her beauty! I was always a little jealous of her when we were growing up."

"No need," the Señora said. "You are quite lovely yourself, my dear. And this is little Gabrielle! How pretty you are, Gabrielle. What a wonderful playmate you'll be for Tabbie."

We picked up her suitcases. Then Ramón met us at the front door of the terminal, and had us wait while he brought the car around. "A chauffeur, Cousin?" she whispered. "Boy, what class!"

"Well, along with the rest of his family, Ramón wears a lot of hats. He is chauffeur, stable hand, gardener, baby-sitter...whatever is needed. The whole family works for Ron. We couldn't do without them. And they are members of the family. Don't dare treat them like servants!"

"Cousin, you fell into a bucket of manure, and came up smelling like roses," my cousin smiled as she repeated the old Southern saying. "We were worried about you when you left. You lost both of your parents so close together, and the three of you had been so close. You said you were going to take a trip, and then we didn't hear from you for months. We had no idea what had happened. What were you thinking, Gail?"

"Scold her good, Rosie," Elfrida said. "If she did that she deserves it. However, in all fairness, you wouldn't believe all of the things which have happened to her, including Ron. And Ron is like a tornado. When he comes into the picture things explode." Her eyes sought mine and we smiled at the scene we remembered in her living room.

"You sound like you know Ron well," Rosie said.

"Oh, I adore Ron. He is like an *hijo* to me—the son I never had."

"Hijo?" Rosie asked.

"Spanish for son," I said.

"I can see I am going to have to get out my English-Spanish translator. I can't wait to meet him. And I can't wait to get caught up on everything which has happened."

"That will take a week at least. I'm glad you came out early, Cousin."

"Well, I'm expecting you to put me to work. Remember, I am experienced in this wedding planning business. I help plan my brothers' and my own. And that was not too many years ago."

"Thank you, and believe me, we will put you to work. The Señora has taken over the orchestration because she knows her way around the local merchants—caterers, florists, dressmakers, etc. But we'll all collaborate. Believe me, I need and appreciate your help."

"Good, that couldn't make me happier."

Tabbie, Maria, and Andy met us when we pulled into Buenaventura. Tabbie flew to me, and I picked her up and gave her a peck on the cheek. She stuck her finger in her mouth and stared at Rosie and Gabrielle with big eyes. I introduced her and Maria to Rosie, who greeted Maria, and then turned to Tabbie. "Something supposed to be wrong with this child?" Rosie asked. "She looks ok to me. And she's absolutely beautiful."

"That we can agree on," I said, giving Tabbie another peck. "And don't be surprised when she calls me Mommy. She started that about the time I agreed to be her Mommy. I adore her."

"I can see why." Rosie had picked up a suitcase, but Ramón took it from her, and disappeared into the house. Rosie looked around the yard out over the ocean. "Oh, Gail, this is so beautiful. I am so happy for you. Will we be able to lure you and Ron and Tabbie to Alabama for some visits?"

We trooped into the house where Marie was firing a volley of Spanish at Ramón, telling him which room upstairs would be Rosie's. Rosie listened for a moment, looked at me, and shook her head. "It just doesn't sound like that high school Spanish, Cousin. Can you keep up?"

"A word here and there, enough to know what is being discussed, but not what is being said about it. But I'm learning."

Marie had made some of her pan dulces, and they were still hot. She poured us coffee as we sat around the kitchen table, and she told Ramón to keep an eye on Tabbie and Gabrielle for us, so we could talk without interruption. I could understand this, and interpreted to Rosie.

"Does Tabbie still have to be watched closely?" she asked.

"Not because of her behavior. She's really a good little girl, seldom makes trouble. But because of other things."

"What other things?"

"Well, you may as well know it now. Ron's wife, Cara died about eighteen months ago. And it may have been murder."

"Murder!"

"Yes."

"Where did it happen?"

"Here. She was pushed off the bluff overlooking the ocean. Places on that bluff are dangerous. At first it was thought that the cliff had crumbled out from under her, but the police now believe it was murder. This has all been unbelievably difficult for Ron, and it precipitated Tabbie's problem. She may have seen the murder. That, of course, was very traumatic for a child. When I arrived, she hadn't spoken since Cara died, and was oblivious to everything around her. She's better now. A lot better. But an attempt was made to kidnap her a few weeks ago. Ron will not allow her to be taken off the grounds. And not out of the house unless someone is with her."

"Oh, wow. I can see what you've been occupied with."

"There's about ten acres here—and we go for walks, but Ramón goes with us, and carries a rifle at the suggestion of the police."

"Why would they want to kidnap her now?"

"Because she is getting past her problem. She is beginning to speak again."

"That's what brought on the illness."

"Exactly."

"I understand now. Imagine trying to explain all of this over the phone or even in a letter! No wonder you didn't communicate."

"And while all of this was happening, Ron was falling in love with Gail, and Gail is trying to keep the relationship as a business arrangement, because she was not sure what his motives were," the Señora said.

"And Mr. Ron, he is pacing the floor, looking out of the window when Miss Gail is playing with Tabbie in the patio. "He think no one knows he is in love, but we are all giggling at him, watching him, wondering how he gonna manage this love affair," Maria said.

"I had heard too much about Hispanic men and their mistresses. I didn't intend to be a victim."

"About which Ron got a big laugh, because from the very beginning he had nothing but marriage on his mind," the Señora said.

"How else could he get a lover, housekeeper, mommy, and teacher for Tabbie all in one? The man may be a rascal, but he's not dumb."

"Speaking of his being a rascal, how did he break down the barrier?" asked Rosie.

"A series of very clever moves," the Señora said. "And a little cooperation from me. I invited them both to our Cinco de Mayo festival held every year at my house next door."

In addition, we told her how Ron had tricked me into letting him be chauffeur to go to Santa Barbara to buy a dress for fiesta, and then tricked me into letting him pay for it.

"The dress was $1500, way over my budget!"

"As he very well knew it would be when you tried it on," the Señora said. "And at Fiesta she looked like a dream in it. Ron couldn't take his eyes off of her. Luis, my stepson asked her to dance with him, and Luis knows all the fancy steps. When she danced in that dress, Ron was watching from the shadows. You didn't know that, did you Hija? Nor did you know that Ron bribed that young lady to cut in and ask Luis to dance with her!"

"Hija? Daughter, right?" Rosie asked.

"Right. No, I did not know any of that. I thought he was still with Loro."

"No." Loro had been detained by some of the young men in her class. When you sat down, he remembered the barbeque outside and made his move. Then he kissed you in the arbor."

"Madre! How do you know about that kiss?"

"Everyone did, Hija. It went on and on. And Ron is a very prominent man in local society, so he was being watched. The servants told me afterward."

I tried to balance my indignation with good manners and forced myself to smile. A furious blush didn't help.

"Ah, so it was the kiss which snagged you." Rosie said.

"Now that you mention it, yes."

"And how was she able to meet you?" Rosie turned to Elfrida.

"I heard that Gail was from Alabama, where my old friend, Goldie Templeton lived," the Señora said. "And that Gail looked very much like Loro—Delores, my other daughter. I suspected that she was the daughter I had given away years ago, and asked to see her. I knew her immediately. And she knew I was her natural mother. Ron eventually got that information out of her, too."

At that moment, we heard a car in the driveway, and looking out I could see that it was Ron. "Here he is now," I said, and rose to go meet him.

"Tabbie, also, had heard the car and came running. "Daddy, Daddy," she shouted, careening through the back door, closely followed by Andy and Gabrielle. I hung back a moment to give him time to greet his daughter.

"Wow," Rosie said. "He's gorgeous. Cousin, I think you hit the jackpot."

"I know I did." We watched Ron alight from the car, and stoop to greet Tabbie, then he turned to Gabrielle, spoke to her a moment and then, lifting each in an arm, brought them through the backdoor where they slid to the floor.

"Hello, I'm inundated with beautiful little girls! And some beautiful big ones, too. Señora! Maria!" He grinned at Rosie, took off his hat, and extended his hand. "I'm Ron.

Welcome to Buenaventura." They shook hands then he turned to put an arm around me and give me a kiss. "What are the four of you plotting?" he asked.

"Almost anything we can get by with," I said. "Sit down. Have some coffee. You took off work early?"

"Yes. Will you bring me some coffee into the study, Querida? I have some things I'd like to go over with you. Excuse me, ladies. And Cousin Rosie, Señora, it's good to have you here. Please make yourself at home. *¡Mi casa es su casa!*"

He left for the back of the house. "Querida?" Rosie said.

"Beloved."

"Ah. I like this guy better all the time."

"' *Mi casa es su casa*'". Did you get that?"

"No."

"An old Hispanic saying. 'My house is your house.'"

"Lovely!"

I took Ron's coffee back to the study. He was seated at his desk, leaning back, his hat on the desk in front of him. I put his coffee down and sat down. "What's up, Querido?"

"Detective Milo dropped by the office awhile ago. The police went by to pick up Michael Garza today. Found him dead."

"What?"

"Yes, dead. Shot. One bullet to his head. I guess I came down too hard on Jorge, Querida."

"Do they think Jorge did it?"

"Who else?"

"If all of this is linked up with drugs, it could have been someone else. But whether it was or was not Jorge, you must not take blame. You didn't kill him. You didn't try to kidnap Tabbie. You didn't take the key to the house out of Sequestra's pocket. You didn't abuse Elfrida."

"Thank you, Querida." I had come around the desk to put my arms around him. He reached up to pull me into his lap and bury his face in my neck for a few minutes. "You make me strong," he said then, and smiled at me. "How does it happen that you are small and look so fragile, but you give me strength?"

"One of those unfathomable mysteries, Querido."

A knock sounded on the door. I started to get up but he held me on his lap. "Come in," he called.

Maria opened the door. "Pardon, Boss, I am interrupting?"

"Oh yes," he said. "Definitely. What did you want?"

"It's Loro. She come over. Wants to see you."

"Oh, that brat!" Loro appeared behind Maria. Ron set me gently off his lap. "Come in Loro."

She came in quickly and sat down. She had been crying. "My daddy is missing," she said. "I can't find him."

"Jorge is missing?" Ron asked.

"Yes."

"Since...?"

"Since that day Mama left with you."

"Did you check with Luis?"

"Yes. Luis hasn't seen him."

"Call his office? Any relatives live nearby he could be with?"

"I've called everywhere and everyone. I can't find him!" She began to cry again.

"We'll have to call the police, Loro." He reached for the phone.

"No! Please, wait!" Ron put the phone down. "I'm in trouble and I need your help."

"What kind of trouble?" Ron asked.

"I've got a habit..."

"Yes. A cocaine habit. Believe it or not, that's old news, Loro."

"You said I had been in rehab and needed to go again."

"Right."

"Maybe I will, but right now..."

"You need a fix."

"Please. I've had nothing for five days! Nothing since Daddy left!"

"Your father was supplying you with cocaine?"

"He hated to see me suffer. I begged and he would give in. He didn't want to do it. I made him!"

"Loro, I don't know where your father is, but I'm worried about you. I would like for you to agree to go to rehab."

"I can't go now!"

"Did you know that your father is linked to some drug dealers? And did you know that one of them, a stable boy by the name of Michael Garza was killed at La Fuente last night?"

"No."

"The police were there this afternoon. Where were you?"

"I've been locked in my room. I haven't answered the door, and I've told our housekeeper not to bother me, not unless my father showed up or called."

"So what are you going to do, Loro? Your father has disappeared. Your supply of cocaine with him. You're refusing to go into rehab."

"Get me some cocaine, Ron."

"No can do. Even if I knew how, I wouldn't. I don't mess around with narcotics."

"But Cara..."

"Cara took care of her own drug habit. I didn't. Did Cara get you started on drugs, Loro?"

"She was so beautiful. And she had you. I thought she knew something, had something I needed."

"Your father was angry about that?

"So angry he wanted to kill her. Maybe he did kill her. I don't know."

Ron looked at me and raised an eyebrow, then turned back to Loro, "You didn't push her off that cliff, did you Loro?"

"Me? Why would I want to get rid of my source for cocaine?"

"How about Luis? He spent a lot of time over here before she was killed. Was he her lover?"

"Oh you are so wrong, Ron. Luis was not her lover. Daddy was!"

"What?"

"Yes. Luis used to come over. In the daytime, with Maria looking over his shoulder. He was just a kid—he's still a kid. And he was fascinated with Cara. Daddy's visits were at night. You were gone too often to that ranch of yours, Ron. He got her into cocaine. He was supplying her habit. Users will do anything for their drug once they have the habit. That's the reason Daddy supplied me with cocaine. He doesn't want me on the streets."

Ron leaned his head on his hands and shook it.

"Oh Loro!" I said. She just looked at me through her tears with that defiant, sullen look.

A long moment passed. Ron raised his head then, looking suddenly tired and beat. "Loro, your mother is staying here with us. You stay with us, too. Don't go back to La Fuente tonight."

"I don't think so. I thought you would help me, Ron."

"No way. If I could I wouldn't."

"You have always been a big brother to me. Big brothers do things for their little sisters because they love them. What you are doing is cruel."

"People have distorted ideas of love these days, Loro. It would not be love to feed your habit. *That* would be cruelty."

"People confuse love with *feel-good*." I said. "Love doesn't always feel good. Sometimes it leads us to the pits of despair. But real love is always right. It never fails."

"Well, then." She got up, turned, and walked out.

A few seconds later we heard the Señora in the hall. "Loro, Loro! Come back. Stay here, Loro." Then the slam of the front door. The Señora came to the door of the office. "Was that Loro? What did she want, Ron?"

"She wanted cocaine, Señora. I told her I couldn't accommodate her."

"Oh!" She sat down and covered her face with her hands. "Why does the Lord make things so hard for us?"

"I don't know, Señora," Ron said. "But Loro just told me her father has not been home since you left the house. And your daughter has just gone out to search for cocaine. We'd better notify Detective Milo and have her picked up for her own safety. She's eighteen?"

"Just turned eighteen."

"Which means she may have to spend the night in jail. Sorry, Señora. We'll see what we can do to keep her out. If we can't, well, it may be good for her." He dialed the number, got Detective Milo and gave him the message.

"Perhaps I should go home," the Señora said. "To be there if Loro returns, or if Jorge shows up."

"No, Señora," Ron laid his hand over hers. "It's dangerous right now. One of your stable boys was killed last night—the same one who got in my house on Fiesta night and tried to take Tabbie. They don't know who killed him."

"Killed! And Loro has been there by herself!"

"Loro is not there now. If she returns home before she is picked up, we'll see that she is in a safe place. The police are watching La Fuente. Stay here. We don't need to have to worry about you as well as Loro. Now let's go and get some dinner. From the smells in the kitchen Maria has fixed chicken enchiladas."

"I can't eat, Ron. I will go upstairs to my room and pray. Hija, will you come with me?"

"Certainly, Madre. Let me go check on Rosie and Tabbie."

Rosie was in the kitchen with Maria. "Hi, Cousin, I'm learning how to make authentic chicken enchiladas."

"Will you be ok, Rosie? I need to go be with the Señora— she has some serious family problems she is dealing with. And keep an eye on Tabbie for me? Ron will be here, too."

"Surely, I'll be glad to keep your gorgeous husband-to-be company. And learn how to make authentic enchiladas. And gaze at the sun sinking over the ocean in your beautiful patio. And look after your beautiful little daughter. But I expect to be filled in on everything when you're able."

"Will do."

CHAPTER XII

Elfrida and I prayed through dinner. Then we began to feel the peace God gives when He is telling you not to worry any longer. The answer---whether yes or no—is in his hands. We knew that things would work out for good. Then we went downstairs. Rosie and Gabrielle, tired after their long trip, and Tabbie, had gone to bed. I went back upstairs to check on them, and found all of them asleep—Rosie in one of the twin beds in her room and Tabbie and Gabrielle in the other. I had been afraid that the little girls would get into little girls giggling fit and keep Rosie up, but all three were sleeping soundly.

Back downstairs I found Ron and the Señora sitting in the patio. I sat down with them to listen to the distant roar of the ocean and feel the cool sea breeze on my face.

"I like your cousin, Querida."

"My best friend for most of my life. We are together for a short time, apart for a long time, and still remain best friends with plenty to share when we see each other."

"How delightful!" the Señora murmured. "I am just beginning to form such friendships with the women in my prayer group."

"I have a few friends like that," Ron said, "but most of them are still in the barrio or in prison."

"Forgive me for speaking of it, Señora," I said, "but Ron, I admired the way you handled Jorge when he became obnoxious."

"Barrio tactics 101," Ron murmured. "Just a little tap. I didn't hurt him."

"I guess there are advantages to being raised in the barrios if you think about it that way," I said.

"A lot of advantages if you use them right," Ron said. "There are things you can learn being raised poor or in difficult conditions which you can learn no other way. Remember that line from *Star Wars*? 'There are things which can be learned only on the dark side!' If the 'dark side' is not doing evil, but is rather tragedy, poverty, abuse or dangerous circumstances, there are many discoveries that can be made. The trouble is that people want to feel sorry for themselves and see only material disadvantages. They forget to look for the gems in those dark caverns."

"Maybe that's the reason Jesus seemed always to be associated with the sick, the troubled, the outcasts," the Señora murmured. "Maybe they are people who had a foot up because of their circumstances, and therefore could learn His difficult lessons better. We get the idea in this life that what we are supposed to be is a success according to worldly standards. I don't think that is necessarily true."

"Maybe this life is to teach us things we need to know for the next," I said. "It doesn't always make a lot of sense otherwise."

"Will you love me in the next life, Querida?" Ron asked.

"There is a line Elizabeth Barrett Browning wrote in a poem to her husband. 'And if God choose, I shall but love thee better after death.'"

"I guess a ghetto or a barrio is a sort of wilderness," the Señora said. "We don't go to the desert in this century like the saints and prophets of the earlier centuries—though it might be good for us if we did. But maybe there are things in modern life which take the place of a desert? After all, a wilderness is a lonely place where one must absolutely depend upon God. The wilderness strips away all conveniences, all artificiality, all hypocrisy. We have such places in modern life, they just aren't called wildernesses. I believe I have been in the wilderness lately, and I am learning some valuable lessons."

"Me too," Ron said.

"And me," I added.

"Almost every great man in the Bible had to spend some time in the wilderness," the Señora said. "Abraham, Jacob, Joseph, David, Elijah, Jesus, John-the-Baptist, Paul to name a few."

"Listen," Ron said. "Do I hear the doorbell?"

"I believe you did. I'll go," I rose from my seat.

"Wait, I'll go too," Ron said, and rose and the Señora rose with him.

Detective Milo was at the door, and with him was Loro. "I believe this young lady belongs here?" the detective said. "The house next door seems to be dark. Nobody home."

"Oh, Loro! Thank God!" Señora said.

"Come in, Detective, come in Loro." Ron stood aside and let them enter, then led them to the den where we all sat down. The Señora sat down by Loro and picked up her limp hand to hold. Loro's face was streaked with tears and she looked near the end of her rope.

"You went out to find some cocaine, Loro. Were you successful?" Ron asked.

"The police picked me up. And I know that it was you who called them," she said as though in complete unbelief that he would do such a thing.

"True enough," Ron said, unperturbed. "So what happened?"

She didn't answer, but Milo spoke up. "Some of the boys found her in a seedy part of town," the detective said. "Nice car, pretty girl, expensive dress and accessories, young. It didn't look good. Some not very savory types were ogling her. We got her for trying to buy narcotics. I was called because they discovered her name is Fuentes and we are working on this case and had been looking for her. By the time I got down to the station they had booked and put her in a cell. I talked them into letting me bring her here. I have some things I want to talk about anyway."

"So do we," said her mother.

"Señora Fuentes, you have been staying at Buenaventura the last few days?"

"Yes. My husband and I were not getting along well, and he had become violent. I can't go home until there is some sort of resolution."

"You have been married for a long time?"

"Twenty years."

"And Miss Templeton is the product of a previous relationship? Both are your daughters?"

"Yes."

"Has Jorge Fuentes been abusive all those twenty years?"

"Not like now. He was often verbally abusive, but not physically violent."

"And the physical violence started when?"

"About two years ago."

"About the time Mr. Fuentes received some news concerning some bad investments?"

"I know little about Jorge's investments, Detective. He is an old-fashioned Hispanic husband who feels that women have no right to involve themselves in family finances."

"Then I will tell you. He did make some bad investments, and NAFTA came in to kick the legs out from under his import-export business. Mr. Fuentes was hurting for money. He got into the business of bringing narcotics into the country from Mexico on his buying trips down there. He became well acquainted with Ron's wife, Cara Casabon. Here is our take on what happened: Ron and Cara were having difficulties and he was away from home a lot. Mr. Fuentes and Mrs. Casabon became close. He introduced her to cocaine and she became addicted. In turn, she introduced his daughter, Loro, the apple of his eye, to cocaine. And she has become addicted. This enraged Jorge. It is our guess that it was he who pushed Cara off the cliff when she told him she was pregnant with his child. Perhaps she demanded money. We don't know."

"Oh please," Elfrida said, breaking into tears. "I can bear no more." She covered her face with her hands and began to sob. I went to her, knelt, and wrapped my arms around her. For a long moment I just held her. And then the tears began to subside and she raised her head, and began to dab at her face with one of those lace handkerchiefs she seems to always carry. .

"Señora," I whispered, "don't lose your courage. We'll get through this."

"Thank you, Hija."

"Just one more thing I might add to this very tragic story," Milo said. "The first Mrs. Fuentes died under mysterious circumstances. She and Jorge were on a trip to the mountains. Jorge had gotten out of the car to take some pictures at a drive-out overview and evidently the brakes slipped and it went off a cliff with the wife in it. Fortunately, they had left their son, Luis, at home. Our concern now is that he might try to harm you, or your daughter, Mrs. Fuentes."

Loro jumped up from her seat. "I don't believe any of this," she shouted. "Daddy would not hurt me,"

"We sincerely hope not."

"Do you know where he is?" she asked. "I've got to talk to him!"

"We'd like to do that too. No, we don't know where he is, but we're looking for him and we will find him."

"How about the young man, Michael Garza, who was killed at La Fuente last night?" I asked. "Who do you think killed him?"

"We're not sure. That's boy's murder was a contract-type killing. Fuente might have done it, or he may have had it done. But the kid had his roots in gangs and the narcotics trade. One of them could have killed him because the narcotics business both the boy and Jorge had been a part of, was collapsing. Jorge is the only one we have not rounded up."

"Maybe he's in Mexico." Loro said. "Maybe he took the plane and..."

"The plane is still in the hanger. Hasn't been moved."

I was still thinking, picturing Cara and Jorge walking together on the cliffs. And Tabbie? Had Cara left her alone in her room, and Tabbie had heard them talking, maybe arguing, shouting at each other, gone to the window, and seen her mother being pushed over the cliff? Perhaps heard Cara's scream, and Jorge had heard Tabbie cry out after he did it?

The Señora had regained her composure. "Detective Milo," she said, "my most heartfelt thanks for bringing my daughter home. Now we would like for you to stay a little longer and help convince this young lady to go into rehab."

Milo turned to Loro. "Loro," he said, "narcotics maim and kill. The whole tragic story of your father, Cara Casabon, the trauma which could have put Ron's little girl in the permanently disabled bracket, the havoc it has wrecked in your own life, is all due to narcotics. And this is just the damage to two families. Multiply that by a hundred and you'll have what I have to deal with during a year. I see it over and over, in family after family in my work."

"Loro," her mother said. "Please listen to him. Please."

Well, I thought. We may as well have that intervention right here, right now. I spoke up. "Loro, we started off all wrong, but when I began to plan my wedding I couldn't get past the idea that you are supposed to be in it—one of my bridesmaids. I would like for us to make a new beginning, be real sisters. I've learned to love Elfrida, and she's taken up a place in my heart right next to the parents who raised me. I want you to be there, too."

Loro began to cry again. "I can't. I don't even like you. You are so goody-two-shoes. You are weird. All of this Christianity stuff. Like Mama. You're a born-again Christian, and I'll never understand that. I doubt that we could ever be close."

"Ok. Not close then. Just be in my wedding. It would mean a lot to your mother and me."

She was still sniffling. "I'll try. Maybe I can. For Mama." Elfrida looked up and smiled at me.

Ron spoke up. "I'd like that Loro. You've always been like a little sister to me. Soon you'll officially be my sister. I know big brothers can be obnoxious, and I probably have been at times. However, big brothers have a lot of real love in their hearts for little sisters, also. And I do for you. I worry about you and I want the best for you. I want you to be in my wedding, and I want you to agree to go to rehab, and make a real try at getting off that stuff you've been taking."

"Well," Loro looked around over the Kleenex she was dabbing her eyes with. "I don't have much choice, do I?"

"No, Loro. You have no choice," Milo said. He got up. "Don't go back to La Fuente, Señora, and Loro." He nodded at each. "Our men will be watching the house and grounds tonight. We want to bring Mr. Fuente in, and we don't want any violence. But one can't be sure about that. We'd like not to have to worry about you."

It was past midnight and we were all in our rooms fast asleep when I heard the pebbles striking the window next to mine. That would be Elfrida's and Loro's window. At first, I thought it was rain, and then I realized it probably wasn't. It wasn't one of California's two rainy seasons.

I got up and moved carefully to the window, keeping the sheer panels in front of me. A man was standing below, and, with a gasp, I realized that it was the same man I had seen standing there before, months ago…and that it was Jorge Fuente.

I heard him call. "Loro," carefully keeping his voice low. Then I heard the window in the room next to mine go up.

"Daddy?"

"Loro, get dressed and come down. We've got to get out of here."

I heard the window close, Loro moving around in the room, and the voice of Elfrida, alarmed, speaking in Spanish, remonstrating with her daughter, pleading and weeping, Loro's angry refusal—also in Spanish. I grabbed my bathrobe and opened the door as Loro in blue jeans ran past, her shoes in her hand. Quickly I knocked on Rosie's door. She quickly poked out a face heavy with sleep.

"Rosie, something's up. I want you and the girls to move across the hall to Tabbie's and my room. Both have deadbolts. Use them!" Rosie, bless her, didn't argue, just nodded, and turned to the sleeping children. Then I flew downstairs to Ron's door. He was up and he opened quickly, evidently having heard something, he had already pulled on his trousers.

"Ron, it's Jorge. He's taking Loro and leaving. We've got to stop them." We ran downstairs to the patio doors and were joined by the Señora in a bathrobe. Loro had stopped to slip on her shoes and now she and Jorge were crossing the lawn toward the cliff. We were opening the patio doors when a police officer with a drawn gun stepped out of the shadows to our left. Ron, who had been dialing 911, hung up.

"Hold it, Mr. Fuente," the police officer said. "Stop right there.!" Instead of stopping, Jorge grabbed Loro's hand and they began to run toward the stairs leading down from the cliff. Elfrida stepped through the patio doors and went after them. Before I even thought about it, I went after Elfrida. And Ron came after me.

"Honey, let the police handle it," he called, but I kept running. This was a woman thing he didn't understand. I had found a mother and a sister, and I wasn't about to let them go. But Ron did understand that I was putting myself in danger. The officer, now behind us, began to yell at us to get down. We were between him and Jorge. Ron tackled me around the waist and we both went down to roll in the grass. He held me down while he whispered in my ear, "You try something like that again, and I will throttle you. Do you understand, Querida?" I had been struggling to get loose, but at his words, my brain clicked into gear, and slowly I nodded. A couple of police officers ran passed us and Ron rolled over and let me sit up.

Jorge and Loro had turned to the path that ran behind La Fuente along the top of the cliff, running toward the boat that was anchored near the steps leading down the cliff. But then, suddenly there were policemen at the other end of that path. Jorge stopped, looked around wildly, grabbed Loro's hand, turned back, and ran squarely into Elfrida. He grabbed Loro around the waist and under the chin. "Oh no! He's going to use her for a hostage," Ron said.

Elfrida began to shout at him. "Let go of Loro, Jorge. Let go of her!"

The police officers had moved in front of Ron and me. "Mrs. Fuente, step aside, please!" one of them shouted.

Elfrida ignored him. "Jorge, everyone knows about you and Cara. Everyone knows you killed her. You will be hunted the rest of your life. Don't make Loro go through a life like that!"

"Oh we have an alternative, Elfrida. We can go off the cliff together." He moved closer to the edge, almost at the spot where Cara had gone over. "You want to watch me throw your daughter from this cliff? You saw what that did to Cara."

"You are an animal, Jorge. You were not able to make an honest living so you turned to dispensing drugs like a common criminal. You ruined Cara, and you ruined your own daughter. And you think I should let you take her with you? Not on a bet!" She slipped off a dainty, pink, feathered, but hard-soled slipper, and hit him hard across the face with it. Momentarily he loosened his hold on Loro who slipped to her knees between them, and began to crawl away. He reached out to grab Elfrida's hair, but she twisted loose and took out a gun she had concealed in her bathrobe pocket. Startled, Jorge stepped backwards and went over the cliff. Elfrida turned around and helped a weeping Loro to her feet. Police officers were suddenly swarming over both La Fuente and Buenaventura, putting their guns away and gathering to look downward over the edge of the cliff. Someone was making a call to the EMS. Ron took my arm, Elfrida took Loro's, and we made our way back to the house.

"I guess I killed my husband. Am I going to go to jail, Hijo?" she asked Ron.

"Not likely. It was witnessed by half the police department and they were all on your side. You had every justification. He was threatening to kill you and your daughter. Where did you get the gun?"

"When Gail and I went into town to the dressmakers, I slipped away to a pawnshop. I had decided Jorge would not torment me again. I'm sorry you had to see that, Gail. I don't know what you must think of me now. Will you still be my daughter?"

"I should turn against you because you had the backbone to stand up to a brute of a husband? No way. You are still my madre."

"Thank you. I do so much need you now. Ron, if they take me in, will you be my lawyer?"

"Certainly."

"It's nice to have a lawyer in the family."

Inside we were met by an excited Rosie. "I saw it all from your window, Gail. The little girls are ok. They slept through everything. I locked them in when I came downstairs. Hope someone has a key."

"Yes, we have a key." Ron said.

She turned to Loro. "Oh my, is this your sister?" She stared into Loro's tear-stained face. "My goodness. You two do look alike. And Elfrida? Congratulations. You won that fight. Is he the man who murdered Cara and tried to take Tabbie? He certainly needed killing."

"He was my husband." Elfrida said.

"Oh, I'm sorry."

"You are right. He needed killing."

Elfrida sat down, looking pale and drained. I got up to make some coffee and Ron got up to answer the doorbell, which was ringing. He returned in a minute with Detective Milo.

"Well, Ron, I guess we can wrap this one up." He sat down.

"Thank the living Lord," I said fervently. "Tabbie will be safe. We can let her play outside and we can go swimming in the ocean."

"Yes, thank you Lord," Elfrida said, "for your watchful care. Detective, am I going to be arrested?"

"I'm not interested in arresting you. I doubt the D.A. will be. He will be too happy to know we've gotten rid of a murderous narcotics gang. We were after the bad guys, and we've got them. Loro, I thought you were going to turn over a new leaf."

"But that was my daddy!" she said, and began weeping again.

"I know Loro, but he was going to kill you," Elfrida said.

"And guess who risked her life to save yours," Ron said. "The mother you never gave much credit to for loving you."

Loro reached toward her mother. Elfrida pulled her down in her lap and spoke softly to her in Spanish, locking her arms around her and rocking back and forth.

"Spanish, the language of love." I smiled at Rosie who was watching everything with wide eyes.

The coffee had finished perking and Rosie and I poured mugs for everyone. Detective Milo took a deep drink and began to make notes and fill out papers. Rosie and I looked at each other. I was suddenly, overwhelmingly, exhausted. I had the impression I was going to faint. "Can Rosie and I go to bed now?" I asked. "I'm beat."

Ron looked at me keenly. "Rosie, go on up," he said. "I'll bring Gail up in a minute."

"Girls will be in Tabbie's room," Rosie said. "I'm going back to mine." She smiled at everyone and left.

"I'm so tired, Querido," I said.

"Delayed reaction. It hits some people that way."

We managed the stairs. Just barely. I was uncertain and wobbly. We stopped at the door to my room while Ron unlocked the deadbolt. I reached up and put my arms around his neck, to kiss him goodnight, and felt myself sinking, slipping down against him. He caught me, picked me up, and carried me to the bed, took off my robe, lay me down, and pulled the coverlet up over me. Then he knelt by the bed and kissed me. "You ok, Querida?"

"I guess so. I guess I'm a wimp after all."

"Anything but. You're a very courageous and loving woman. Too courageous and loving for your own good. I'm going to have to watch you carefully."

I grasped for his hand. "Stay with me, Ron, just a little while."

"I'll be here, Querida." I heard him pull up a chair, and then oblivion.

It was late when I woke. I could tell because the sun was high in the sky. I sat up and looked around. It was a tap on the door that had awakened me, and I heard it again. "Come in."

Rosie opened the door with one hand, and was holding the tray against her side with the other. "Hi, Kiddo. Ron said let you sleep. But at ten o'clock we decided you need some breakfast."

"Oh, is it ten o'clock? What kind of a hostess am I?"

"A tired one. Seems like you've been under a strain for quite awhile—trying to juggle caring for Tabbie, preparing for a wedding, the whole Fuente thing. Lots of brides fall out, and most don't even have to deal with kidnappings and murders." She sat the tray down on the bedside table. Taquitos and cantaloupe, with two cups of coffee—one for Rosie, one for me.

"The children?"

"Been up since seven. Ron sat with you until they woke, then he took them downstairs for Maria to feed, and me to dress. She called Ramón to come and watch them. I got up at eight. Loro and Señora are still asleep. The detective kept them up pretty late."

"Jorge?"

"Dead. The fall killed him."

"Ron?"

"Went to work. He's worried about you. Wants you to call him on his private line at his office. Here's his cell phone. Just punch redial."

I did and heard his voice. "Hi, Ron."

"You ok, Querida?"

"I think so. Thanks for staying with me."

"My pleasure. Are you sure you shouldn't see a doctor?"

"I believe I'm all right."

"Then take it easy today, ok?"

"You didn't get any rest."

"Slept in the chair."

"That's not much rest. Don't work too hard."

"Ok. Don't worry about me."

"That's my privilege. Bye, Ron."

"Bye, Querida."

We heard the door to the room next to us open, close, and then Loro opened our door and peered in. "Hi, Loro,"

Rosie said. "Come in and sit down." To our surprise, Loro came in and sat down on the other bed.

"Is she sick?" she asked Rosie.

"Hey, she talks. Ask her."

"Just overdid, Loro," I said. "Thought I was superwoman. Turned out I'm not."

"I kind of know the feeling."

"Maybe we're more alike than we thought."

Uneasily, she turned back to Rosie. "You're from Alabama?"

"Yes."

"Is it pretty there? Is it like California?"

"It's pretty, but it's not like California. The two states are just about opposites. Alabama is traditional. Maybe too traditional. California is often modern and liberal. Probably too modern and liberal. California is desert and mountains. Alabama's is a different kind of beauty. Lots of hardwood everywhere. Big trees—oak, sweet gum, magnolia, pine. In the small town where Gail and I were raised there are a lot of old houses—mostly brick or frame, some of them left from the Victorian era. It's rolling hills, particularly in the north. Homes are farther apart because there is less population and more acreage there to build on. Cities and towns are not so crowded. People are more laid back, relaxed. There's a lot of common courtesy. The lady with you in the grocery line is likely to start a conversation, and it's rude not to join in. And if you do you'll probably be glad you did because she's likely to share a new recipe she's trying with you."

Loro hesitated, staring at the floor. "It sounds nice." She waited a minute and then stumbled on. "I've got to get out of here. I've got to get away. I wonder if I applied to go to college there, if it would be all right. I mean…I don't know anyone who's not from here but you. And I'd like to go somewhere where I kind of know someone."

"How are your grades, Sweetie?"

She blushed and looked at the floor. "Not too good."

"I understand you've signed up for rehab."

"Yes."

"You're not going to be able to get in any but a local college with C's and D's. I'll tell you what. Go to rehab. Get your narcotics problem straightened out. Take a year or two of community college and then transfer to the University of Alabama or Auburn. They will probably take you as a transfer and upper division student. Then you can come to Alabama and, if you like, we will be your family there. You can visit us, or the family farm on weekends and holidays. If you do the chores like the rest of us have to do on the farm, you can spend vacations there. How does that sound to you?"

"I don't know if….."

"Take it Loro," I said. "It's a great offer, the best offer you've had or will get. Take it. I can vouch for the fact you'll have the time of your life with our relatives there. You'll find a new life there."

"I don't know if Mama…."

"Mama will be for anything that will make you happy and get you away from the old crowd," I said.

"I've been badgering Ron to bring Gail and Tabby for Christmas. Come with them then. You can look things over for yourself."

"Thank you. I'll do that. It sounds nice. You sound nice."

"Sometimes I am," Rosie smiled. "I could try to sell you on swimming parties down at the river, ice cream get-togethers, Fourth of July picnics, but maybe I'd be painting too good a picture. You also have to put up with my father's crankiness when it comes to the right way to shovel the horse manure out of the stables, and my mother's bossiness when you help her can tomatoes. They will also make you go to church with them. But if you think you might like it, plan to come."

"Horse manure? Canning? Ugh! And church....I dunno. I just don't dig this God thing. But I just can't think God has done too much for me."

"You'd be surprised how good shoveling horse manure and canning tomatoes will be for you. But as for God? Well, I can see your point," Rosie said. "He hasn't brought your grades up or fixed your home life, and we realize that has been pretty awful. Just because you live in a beautiful spot in the greatest nation in the world and enjoyed a privileged upbringing by parents who evidently adored you. I can see why you might feel deprived."

Loro dropped her eyes. "Daddy is dead." Rosie rose to put her arm around Loro. "That's rough. That's really rough. We're sorry

"And the police were after him. He was into dealing narcotics."

"I'm sorry, Kiddo. But remember, whatever you father did, he loved you dearly. And remember this, too. You were in no way responsible for his death. His life and the way it played out was put into effect long before you came along."

Loro began to sob in earnest and buried her face in Rosie's shoulder. "I just can't stay here and face my friends when they find out about it. No one will want to be with me or invite me to anything."

Rosie hugged her and patted her shoulder. "Maybe that's good. You need to get a new life, Loro. You can do that. If you'd like to be part of our family, we would love to help you."

"Thank you. Maybe I could learn to be more like you and Gail."

"Be yourself. But welcome to the sisterhood."

"And don't discount your mother," I said. "She's a great lady."

"Amen to that," Rosie said.

"Speaking of whom," I said, "is she ok, Loro?"

"Tired. Very tired. She said she was going to keep to her bed for awhile."

"Ok. I'll shuffle over to see her when I get up."

"Come on downstairs with me, Loro," Rosie said. "First lesson on being an Alabama girl. You're expected to be a good cook. Maria is fixing *chile rellenos*. Let's go learn how."

When they left I rose and pulled on some blue jeans. I needed to see Tabbie. But first I wanted to see the Señora. I knocked and she called for me to enter

She was in bed, but had on her robe. She started to sit up but I crossed over and pushed her back down on the pillow. "How are you, Madre?"

"Not bad. Just tired."

I leaned over to kiss her forehead. "That makes two of us."

"Ron told us last night you collapsed at your door, and he had to put you to bed."

"I can't hide a thing from you, Madre."

"Loro stopped by your room?"

"Yes. Rosie was visiting, and she stopped by to talk to her."

"I think she blames me for everything. I think she hates me, and I'm afraid she will never get over it."

"I don't think she likes either of us too much right now. Just give her time. She's still a teen ager. And it will take time to get past the effects of the narcotics."

"But she's my baby…"

"I know it's tough, but you've got to let her go, soon. She has to learn to fly. Legally, she's an adult."

"I guess I'm going to be alone."

"No, you have Ron, me, and Tabbie, right next door."

"How will I ever manage? I know nothing about running things. I don't even know what Jorge paid the men who worked for him. Jorge didn't believe in women knowing about the business end of things."

"Ron will help. Jorge kept books, bank records, all of those things, I'm sure. Ron will help you go through them, and make whatever decisions you need to make. That stuff, which seems so difficult to you and I, is easy for a lawyer."

"My name is on no bank accounts."

"You'll manage. I have a hunch you have a lot of hidden business talent. I've seen the way you handle things like the Cinco de Mayo celebration and also my wedding plans. By the way, don't think you have to keep on helping with that. You probably are not up to it…."

"Oh please, Hija, let me. As soon as I can get on my feet, I'll need to keep busy. It will help me get past all of this, and convince me I still have a daughter even if Loro doesn't choose to be one."

"Why…If you are sure you're up to it."

"Let me try. I'll let you know if I start to cave in."

"I'll need to get on my feet again also. Ron said I had a delayed reaction from all that happened."

"I guess you inherited that from me, along with the blonde hair and blue eyes."

"You've experienced this before?"

"All my life. Do just fine during a crisis, and collapse afterward."

"Madre, how did Jorge know what room Loro was in? He threw pebbles at your window."

"He has powerful binoculars in his boat. Probably kept far enough out in the water so the police did not notice. We don't draw curtains on the ocean side, since usually no one is out there."

"I see. When is Loro going to rehab?"

"Tomorrow morning. Ron has made arrangements already. He also made arrangements for her to be back here temporarily for your wedding."

"I'm glad." I rose to go.

"Read the Bible to me before you go, Hija."

"Ok," I picked up the Bible by the side of her bed. "Old or New Testament?"

"New Testament. Fourteenth chapter of John."

I turned to the great comfort chapter, the words Jesus left his disciples before His crucifixion. "'Let not your hearts be troubled. Ye believe in God. Believe also in me…'" The Lord's ancient words to a people soon to be bereft of His presence. We finished the chapter, and then we prayed together.

"Can I bring you some breakfast?" I asked.

"Not now. Maybe later I will have something."

"Go back to sleep, Madre." I kissed her again.

Downstairs I was rewarded by my daughter's delight in seeing me. She came running to hug my knees and I reached down to pick her up. Gabriella looked up and smiled, and Ramón grinned at me from the loveseat. "Thank goodness you are here, Miss Gail. She's been 'Mommying' us all to death."

"Gabby play," she said.

"Gabby is playing with you, Tabbie?" I hadn't noticed the rhyme before. I sat down on the sofa leaving space for Gabrielle to sit with us.

"Gabby is playing with Tabbie," she said, and giggled and clapped her hands.

"Oh, that sounds nice. Like a poem." I put my arm around Gabrielle. "Do you like California, Gabrielle?"

"I like California." She smiled.

"Are you and Tabbie and Letty going to be my flower girls?" I asked.

"Yes, flower girls!" Tabbie shouted, and both girls broke into giggles and crawled off of the sofa to resume a game of cutting up old magazines on the floor.

"Have they been good today, Ramón?"

"Very good, Miss Gail. I've gotten in a lot of TV watching."

"Thanks for the help. I've been a little under the weather."

"Too much excitement."

"Yes. Too much excitement. I'm sorry Sequestra's friend was killed."

"He was not a good man." Ramón shook his head. "I told her, but she wouldn't believe me. He would have sidetracked Sequestra. Probably she would not have finished high school."

"I'm glad she's going to finish. You're a good brother, to keep an eye on her, Ramón. You're going to the University, I hear."

"Yes!" he smiled widely. "I won a scholarship!"

"That's so great, Ramón. You know that Loro will probably be going to junior college."

"Is she? I'm glad."

"Maybe you can show her the ropes. She could use your help."

"Miss Snobbish need my help? I don't think so."

"Miss Snobbish, huh!" I looked up to see Loro and Rosie standing in the doorway behind Ramón. Rosie was trying to hide a smile. Loro had hands on her hips, eyes blazing. Ramón stood up hastily.

"Gosh. I didn't know you were here. I mean, I'm sorry."

"What makes you think I'm snobbish?"

"Well, just because we live next door and you've never spoken to me, you put your nose in the air when we were in high school, and wouldn't return a 'hi'. I guess I was just judging too hastily."

"Yes, you were," she said.

"You're starting junior college this fall?"

"Probably."

"Well, uh, I'll see you around."

"Look, I'm sorry I was snobbish. I'm trying to change."

"I'm, uh, sorry about your father. That was rough."

She looked at him with tears trembling in her eyes and sat down on the loveseat. He sat down beside her. She began to cry, and he awkwardly put an arm around her. I looked up at Rosie, who raised her eyebrows and nodded toward the door. I followed her out. Tabbie and Gabrielle were still deeply engrossed in cutting up magazines. We slipped out to the patio.

"Who would have thought…Ramón?" I asked.

"He may be just what she needs. At least right now, to anchor her. He's a smart kid. Level head. Cheerful worker.

And you know what's going to happen among her snobbish friends when word gets out about her father."

"That will be the end, for her, of social life. She'll be a lonely little girl."

"Except for Ramón."

"Hmmm. Wonder how he'd look in a fancy western suit? Ron needs another usher for the wedding."

"Perfect!" She gave me a high five.

Maybe things were looking up.

CHAPTER XIII

Gail asked me, Rosie, to write this, the final chapter of hers and Ron's love story. "There is so much—I'm still trying to assimilate it." She said. "It was as though I was in the eye of a hurricane—things were going on around me but too fast for me to comprehend. I didn't have a good view."

That may be. It was obvious to everyone from the very beginning; theirs was a very intense and beautiful love story. Although he showed doubts about her faith, in the beginning, I believe what he said later about God bringing Gail three thousand miles because both he and Tabbie, as well as Señora Elfrida so needed her was true. Ron's heart had been crushed. He had been raised in the Christian faith, but when his wife betrayed him, his marriage went sour, his daughter became ill, he went through one of those dark nights of the soul and his faith slipped. But then God sent Gail. Love truly called her across the miles. Of course, at first, he taunted Gail about her "born again" status—and Gail put him down as a non-believer. Much to his own regret, because he was falling in love with her.

Gail is of average height, but gives the impression of being petite. Though very strong, she appears to be delicate. The fact that she stood firm in her conviction not to marry outside of her Christian faith probably saved them both a world of heartache, and gave Ron the rare privilege, not given to many, to hear from God, personally.

After that terrible night at La Fuente when Jorge died, Loro left for rehab as she had promised her mother she would do. She showed some of her mother's and sister's courage by putting aside the weeping she had been doing and holding her chin up and her shoulders back, giving each of us a kiss before she left, even Gail. Whether she has ever been able to get past her love for Ron, none of us will ever know. She has never brought up the subject, and, of course, we do not ask. She wanted only Ramón to drive her to the destination, which was in a neighboring small town. He returned looking both happy and sad—that their friendship had finally blossomed when they were separated.

Ron was home the following Saturday when my parents came into the Los Angeles airport, so the three of us, Ron, Gail and I drove down to meet them. They came up the ramp with that "deer caught in headlights" stare and the bewildered expression people have when they have landed in a completely alien place. Mama kept that expression during most of her stay. Daddy covered his apprehension with bluster. We took them for coffee before starting the trip back, and Gail and I exchanged secret looks of amusement as we watched Daddy and Ron do the emotional circling dance that two alpha males do when meeting for the first time. But they soon set that side and decided they liked each other. Back at Buenaventura they would lean back in easy chairs and discuss the relative merits of Charolais and Black Angus cattle, and whether Ron should experiment with irrigation and put in a few acres of oranges or a farm crop, on his ranch.

And, of course, they included in the conversation all of those deeply intriguing (to males) matters such as soil testing and appropriate farm vehicles. As for Mama, she had never been happy too far away from a kitchen, so she hung around Maria watching her make a never-ending supply of pan dulces and bunuelos (for visiting wedding guests) until she could very capably make them herself, and free Maria for other work.

I loved the Señora from the start. What's not to love? Her elegance, her dignity in the face of the tragedies which had shadowed her life, her iron courage, her ability to admit her weaknesses and vulnerability, and her devotion to the Lord made an irresistible combination. She remained at Buenaventura for a few days after Jorge's death, seeing to the quiet cremation and scattering of ashes over La Fuente, the many tasks connected to insurance and bank matters (with Ron's careful guidance), and then she insisted on returning to her own home, announcing with authority that the wedding reception would be held there, since she was the mother of the bride. Besides that, it was a practical suggestion. La Fuente was larger and had a ballroom. It turned out that Jorge, despite his many obvious faults, had not left her too badly off. There was sizable life insurance policy taken out years before. And aside from that, the Señora announced that now she would take up a career, and it would be catering and wedding receptions. Gail's and Ron's would be the first of many receptions held there.

In addition to her love affair with Ron, Gail had found an additional great love in her life. That was her love for the Pacific Ocean. As soon as they could be sure it was safe, she and Ron took Steve, my husband, who had driven out, the girls, Tabbie and Gabbie, and me for a beach party.

Beach parties are old hat to Gail and me. Alabama also has beautiful beaches—long, wide, flour-white sand and seductive warm waters. Both Gail and I are strong swimmers and, as young girls, we would spend hours at Gulf Shores, Alabama, both in the water and sunning on the blinding white sand. The Gulf is a gentle lover; for the most part it is quiet. It slips in from the Caribbean, bringing intoxicating balmy breezes on summer nights. It laps playfully at your boat or dock, and rocks you gently in its embrace. Of course it has its temperamental times when, with hurricanes, it goes berserk, and destroys everything in its path. Its rages are momentous. But its normal temperament is calm and soothing.

Not so the Pacific. In spite of its name, the Pacific is a passionate lover. It entices with its great beauty, plunges you into icy water, pounds you, tumbles you, roars, sings, croons, and is altogether addictive. I learned to love it too, in the short time I was there. The beach party was a great success for the grownups. And the little girls were paddling in shallow water and building sand castles, having the time of their lives.

Lupe, Ron's married sister, her little daughter, Letitia, and Anna, his sister bridesmaid-to-be drove down both to see us and for dress fittings. I liked both women, and so did Gail. Lupe has that interesting combination of the romantic and no-nonsense business sense Latin women achieve so easily. She has a small dress shop, started in a flea market, and doing pretty well in a small shop in a popular mall.

Two days before the wedding, the groom's dinner was held at Ron's ranch. It was not a sit-down dinner. It was, of course, a barbeque. And it was very well attended. All who were invited to the wedding were invited to the barbeque. A few days before that, my brothers had arrived from Alabama with their wives and children. They had all been lapping up the relaxation, the pool, horseback riding, and eating ranch victuals with the hired hands. They loved it. Ron, Gail, and I had driven up to meet them and make them welcome. We were able to spend only an hour or so before we had to hand them over to Carlos, the ranch foreman and return to Buenaventura.

I have come to the conclusion that Alabamans and Latinos are not as different as one might first suspect. Both are family-oriented. Both are strong and deeply prejudiced advocates of their own culture. Both are often blind to their need for change. Both are proud of their often violent histories. Both appreciate the separate and equally important roles of men and women, which, at its best makes the sexes strong and secure in who they each are, and, at its worst, lapses into male dominance and female subservience.

Americans not from that region think of the Deep South as a part of the country settled by Northern Europeans, their culture cast in iron and inflexible, their prejudices against other races and nations fixed. Actually, there is a lot of mixed blood there, which has lived peacefully intermarrying for decades. We forget that Spain and Portugal are actually not far from Ireland and England, and that Columbus and Vasco de Gama were early explorers, neither of whom were northern Europeans. In the South, along with the Templetons and Dixons, you will find the Cuevas, Dedeaux and Ladiners, and even a few Kesslers and Stanislowskis, and there are Goldbergs and Kaplans, none of which raised any eyebrows in my hometown.

In one of her books, Agatha Christie wondered publicly why American women seem to all have cat faces. Because we did not kill all the Indians when we settled the country, Agatha! We married a good many of them. And those pure ethnic genes resulted in generations of straight dark hair and high cheek bones, slightly slanted eyes---as the great mystery writer said---cat faces. Most old American families which helped settle this country have some Indian blood, including my own, and that is where I get my high cheek bones and straight dark hair.

All of which is why Southerners, Southwesterners, and Latinos share an instinct for good barbecue—having cooked over campfires so long in our recent past. Ron's barbecue was among the best.

The men of the ranch had dug a huge hole, and built a fire in it. When the fire burned down to coals, they wrapped a large piece of cow in something damp and lowered it into the hole, over the coals, covered it and let it cook most of the night before the barbecue.

For our part, Mama and Maria whipped up a ton of ranch-style beans. Mama used about a bushel of potatoes and innumerable eggs for potato salad. Gail and I should know. We were drafted to peel the potatoes and shell the eggs. And for dessert we had self-made sundaes for all the children and any adults who cared to indulge, with a choice of hot fudge, bbutterscotch or strawberry, topping, sprinkles, nuts, whipped cream, etc. I stopped counting how many children there were.

There was Tabbie, who forgot she was supposed to have a neurosis, and enjoyed running games of hide and seek and jumping in the pool with her Latino and Alabama cousins, my Gabbie, little Lettie, and Ron's younger brothers who didn't think it damaged their maleness to be told to look out for the younger children. Some of the Señora's prayer group partners brought children and grandchildren. Well, I could go on and on. It was a night to remember, complete with a guitar one of the ranch hands had brought, and who played and sang both Latino and Country-Western songs very well.

Back at Buenaventura, the days resumed in a flurry of florist visits, dressmaker visits, calls to musicians, and innumerable phone calls, all of which had to be answered. The Señora, glad to be busy in a new life and resolutely putting aside the old one, took over the responsibility of the rehearsal dinner and the music and catering for the wedding. Of course, she had the help of her prayer group partners, all of whom seemed to be enjoying pitching in. And of course they were added to the guest list, along with husbands and children.

We had rented chairs to seat one hundred. But it soon appeared the guest list would exceed that number. I told Ron and Gail the mayor's wife had called and expressed a desire to attend with her husband. They both shrugged and said, "Invite them."

I told them there were no seats left. They shrugged again. "Tell them they will have to bring their own!" It was their day, and they refused to be perturbed.

I said, "We'd better hang out a SRO sign."

Ron just said, "Probably a good idea," and dismissed the whole thing from his mind. As I said, I like that man.

The morning of the wedding, I took Gail's breakfast up to her. "This is the last time, Sweetie," I said, "unless your first babies are twins or something. Now you owe me a couple of breakfasts in bed."

"Ah, Cousin, you are wonderful, and I certainly will return the favor. At your next wedding. Meanwhile you're a dear and I love you forever."

She had barely finished when Ron pushed in. "Mr. Casabon, you are out of order," I said sternly. "You are not supposed to see the bride before your wedding on the wedding day."

"Tough," he said. "I just wanted to make sure she was still here—hadn't run away during the night or something." He was smiling at her his wonderful smile and she was smiling back a bit tenuously. "I can't believe I've actually snagged her. I keep getting scared she'll cut lose and fly away."

"Get out of here, Mr. Casabon," I said. "I promise to deliver her all in one piece and on time."

He left with no further argument and still grinning. Gail had barely gotten dressed when the Señora and Loro appeared. The Señora was on Cloud Nine, with both of her daughters with her in the same room, and Loro apparently calm and agreeable. She expressed a desire, as the only parent remaining in Gail's life, to pray for Gail and give her a parent's blessing.—a very ancient rite that has been resurrected among modern Christians in the last few decades. Probably many marriages would go better if it were used more often. We all prayed for Ron and Gail then. And I remembered how Gail and the Señora had prayed through the dinner hour for Loro when she ran away to the streets, and how God had wondrously intervened and brought her safely home.

Perhaps if God were invited to more weddings our divorce rate would decline.

Before the Señora and Loro left to see that the reception area was progressing according to plan, Ron's sisters, Lupe and Anna with Letitia came in. The room was getting crowded and I decided to move everyone downstairs. Lupe's husband a few other of Ron's male relatives were in the room and I shooed them out, brought the women in where we could talk, and compare notes. The Señora made it her business to become acquainted with Ron's grandmother and she invited his family to spend the night with her at La Fuente after the wedding, since they would have to return to Santa Barbara late and in heavy traffic.

The house began to fill up with people Gail and I did not know well. Hispanic babble was everywhere. It was making us dizzy. We grabbed a taco each from the kitchen and escaped upstairs, after checking on Tabbie and Gabbie, who were playing in the patio under the watchful eyes of Ramón, whom Loro was keeping company. Eventually Letitia, Miguel, Ricardo, and Roberto joined the little girls in the patio. The yard was ringing with children's laughter and children's voices. (Have you ever listened to children at play, just listened to the sound without trying to translate into words? It is one of the prettiest sounds on earth.) But sensible Señora, immediately alarmed, and Detective Milo, who had come to attend the wedding, immediately sent one of his men to the cliff to make sure no one accidentally went over, and none of Jorge's crowd was still hanging around.

Gail and I sat for a while and just watched them from her window. Finally, I left to take my bath and get dressed in my bridesmaid's dress. When I returned Gail had also bathed and was lying down. "I'm beat," she said.

"Take a nap," I said. "I'll keep everyone away."

She closed her eyes, but almost immediately there was a knock on the door. "The florist is here. Where do we put the flowers?"

"See Señora Fuentes," I said.

Another knock again in ten minutes. "Where do the bridesmaids and flower girls change?"

"My room, across the hall."

Another knock a few minutes later. "Would you like coffee?"

"No."

Another knock. "Should I give Tabbie her bath now?"

"Yes. In the room across the hall."

Another knock, "What should we do about the dog, Andy, during the ceremony?"

"His invitation is official. Let him attend."

Finally we gave up on trying to rest and just sat by the window and watched the comings and going below us, talking girl talk. And then it was four o'clock. Gail had refused a professional make-up job (she really didn't need it) and opted for her everyday dress-up face. She had been putting a peach satin polish on her toenails and fingernails. I sat watching her and thinking how pretty she is. Her hair is not fine and silky like most blond hair. It is gloriously thick, with a natural wave, which makes it turn under just at her shoulders. She wears light bangs, and her face is full, her chin firmer than one would expect with those eyes and hair. Her figure is exquisite. Along with her beauty, she gives an impression of capability and friendliness. And I saw something else which I had never seen before—a faint suggestion of the Hispanic in her full lips and pretty profile. As she painted her fingernails, I saw a tremor in her hand.

"Nervous, Gail?"

She smiled. "A little. Who wouldn't be? There are going to be a lot of people down there, Rosie."

"That's what you get for marrying a prominent man like Ron."

"Sometimes I wish he were a bank clerk or a carpenter."

"A lot of bank clerks' and carpenter's wives would trade places with you."

By five thirty we were both dressed and had all of our hair and makeup in place. We heard another knock on the door."

"Who is it?"

"Ron."

"Go away, Ron," I teased him.

"I want to see my bride."

"Too bad. Not available right now." I opened the door to grin at him, and he pushed his way in. Gail was standing by the window in her wedding dress, looking unbelievably lovely. He stopped and drank her in with his eyes, said something in Spanish, and went over to kiss and hold her a few minutes.

He looked rather wonderful himself. He was dressed in an off-white western suit, with a pale turquoise shirt and a bolo tie, set off with a large turquoise. His presence filled the room.

"Ron, you are so handsome!" she said.

"And you are so beautiful, Querida. Did I ever tell you that?"

"Once or twice." She was leaning on his shoulder and I saw a flash of apprehension pass over her face. "Will I be a good wife, Ron?"

"Of course. If you're not, I'll beat you."

She giggled. "But I'm awfully independent."

"And I hope you will continue to be, Querida."

"Will you be a good husband?"

"Of course. You'll make me be."

"We'll have differences."

"Querida, when a husband and a wife agree on everything, one of them isn't needed. Of course, we will have differences. We'll talk them over. Sometimes we will get mad at each other. All kinds of things will happen. That's life. Bring it on. We'll face it together. And we have the Lord. The three of us are an unbeatable combination."

"Thank you, Ron. I love you."

"And I love you. Oh, I almost forgot what I came for. He took a small box out of his pocket and opened it. In it, lay an exquisite turquoise necklace, in gold, set off with pearls. "I thought you might like this for your 'something blue'. When I saw it I thought of you, Querida, because of those turquoise eyes of yours."

"Oh Ron, it's beautiful!"

He lifted the necklace out of the box and she turned so he could fasten it around her neck. She turned back around so he could admire it on her, and he smiled. "Lovely!"

"Thank you, Ron."

"Not for you, Querida, for me. To see a beautiful necklace on a beautiful woman."

She laughed at some private joke they shared, I guess, and he caught her up for another kiss.

We were hearing music from below, preambles to the wedding march. "I'd better go," he said.

"Yes, you'd better go," I said. I turned around to find the bridesmaids, Maria and the Señora had quietly gathered watching the love scene. They backed up to let Ron through.

Gail turned for a final look in the mirror, retouched her lipstick, took a deep breath, and said, "Let's go."

We stopped and picked up our flowers in the hall below. Outside, the yard was packed with people. Where did they all come from? I wondered, as Anna, and then Loro walked down the aisle. I came next, holding a small exquisite bouquet of white sweetheart roses. Tabbie came next, scattering rose petals, lifting them out one by one, and examining each carefully before she dropped it. She was followed closely by Andy, smiling his doggie smile and, wagging his tail, seemingly at everyone. Gabbie and Letitia were grabbing handfuls of petals and scattering them, throwing a few at each other in the process. And then came Gail, holding the Señora's hand on one side, her uncle's arm on the other. And when the minister asked, "Who gives this woman in marriage?" My dad with his innate dignity and graciousness (which always makes me proud), said "Señora Fuentes and I do." And they both stepped back and took their seats.

Gail took Ron's arm and he clasped his hand over hers. My eyes wandered to Ramón, whom I had been thinking of as a sort of house boy. But I realized at that moment that he was not a boy any longer. Although young, he was very much a man, and a handsome man. He was looking at Loro, with something in his eyes I could not quite interpret. Concern? Love? Vexation? All three? I glanced at Loro, who had smiled briefly at him, and then fixed her gaze on the ground. What was she thinking? She was unreadable.

And then they had said their vows. Ron, who had never cared about hiding his feelings, good or bad, was giving Gail the post-wedding kiss—possibly a duplicate of that arbor kiss which had become the talk of the town because it went on so long people in the audience started whistling and cheering. I borrowed Gabbie's basketful of petals and began to throw them at the bride and groom. And soon Loro did the same with Tabbie's. Ron finally let Gail loose, but buried his face in her hair for another few seconds (was I the only one who could see his lips move in prayer as he thanked God for his bride?) before she could turn around and start the trip back up the aisle. Ron reached down to pick Tabbie up on one arm, and Gail took his other, Andy following closely behind. People were laughing and cheering and wiping tears from their eyes. I held onto Gabbie's hand and Loro took Letitia's so the little girls would not get lost in the crowd, and we made it back to the house.

Ron and Gail had opted not to have a reception line. "They are long and boring," they said. And no more than a half dozen posed photographer's pictures. "Taking an hour to pose for pictures creates a vacuum in festivities," they said. Instead, we all went next door for the Señora's reception and refreshments. No alcoholic beverages, but some lovely fizzy drinks, along with the Señora's buffet loaded with both

Hispanic and Alabama delicacies. I was happy to see that Mama was pouring coffee and tea, which gave her a special place of honor. Afterward the musicians took turns playing and everyone danced. I was delighted to see Luis dancing. Gail had told me what a wonderful dancer he was, and he proved to be.

In all of the confusion, Ron and Gail seemed to just disappear. Steve, whom I had not been able to be with much since he had driven out, danced with me, and it was like our courtship days. I sincerely hoped that Ron and Gail would be as happy as we had been, and I had the secure feeling they surely would. Not only was it great love on both sides, it was the right kind of love. Afterward Steve and I stepped out to stroll around Buenaventura and La Fuente grounds. A romantic setting for an evening of high romance. The sun was just setting into a spectacular sunset. As we walked toward the water, we found Ron and Gail sitting on a couple of the folding chairs in the dusk, watching the sun sink into the ocean.

"Ron, are you not going to take your bride on a honeymoon?" I asked.

""Oh yes," Ron said. "But we decided to watch the sunset first."

"I believe God decorated the sky this evening especially for Ron and me," Gail said. "Do you think He does such things, Rosie?"

"I don't doubt it for a minute. Where are you going on your honeymoon?"

"Ask Ron. He never tells me anything."

"I've just now been able to persuade her not to take Tabbie along," he said.

"But she needs me," Gail said.

"She'll be ok. Maria, Sequestra, and Ramón will be looking after her. And the Señora is in seventh heaven in her new role as grandmother. She's already got plans for visits to the ice cream parlor and the children's section of the library. Next it will be Disneyland and Marineland, I suppose."

"No doubt," Steve said.

"Rosie, you were tops, I could never have made it without you."

"Glad to be of service," I stooped to kiss her, then Ron. "It's a one-time only thing, though. Next wedding, hire someone else. See you at Christmastime?"

"We'll plan on it. That sounds good," Ron said. The men shook hands and we left them.

We later learned that Ron's destination was Puerta Vallarta. Gail made him come back early so they could pick up Tabbie and spend the remainder of their honeymoon at Ron's ranch.

EPILOGUE

It has been two years since our wedding. And ours is still a wonderful love affair. Do we have differences? Oh, many. One of our big differences is that I am anxious to get back to my field of helping exceptional children, because I love it. But Ron wanted me to stay with Tabbie and any other children we have until they are in school. I found he was right about Tabbie. Today she is a normal, healthy little girl, but occasionally the dark shadows creep back and she has nightmares and anxiety attacks. At such times, she needs me to be with her for extra care and cuddling, and I am thankful I am there for her, and not at work. She is in the first grade and doing well, equally at home in both Spanish and English, and getting along with teachers and peers.

Have I learned Spanish? Well, not as well as Tabbie. They tell me that God put a special little switch in children's heads. When it is on, they can pick up language easily. But it gradually turns off as we age, so it is more difficult. If I had my way about it, Spanish would be taught in the first five grades in public school, especially in Border States. We would have a bi-lingual nation, and both Anglos and

Latinos would understand each other better, and perhaps we, in the United States, would become more international in our outlook. However, I am not completely left out when our Hispanic relatives and friends converse in Spanish. I can understand most of it, and carry on an acceptable conversation.

Loro has been free of drugs during these two years. She spent last year at the University of Alabama, and took her vacations with my family in Alabama. I don't know if she will ever return to Carpentaria and her mother's home. She communicates very little with her mother, hardly at all with Ron and me. I wish I could understand and relate to my little sister better, but she politely holds me at a distance. Surprisingly, however, she relates very well to my family in Alabama, especially Rosie. And Rosie tells me that a new Loro is emerging from the old cocoon.

Nevertheless, she and Ramón remain close, and he is good for her. During her freshman year at the local junior college, they were together every day. He is in his pre-med course at UC at Santa Barbara. He wanted very much for her to stay in California and go to school with him, but she made the decision to get her degree from Alabama. Where is that relationship going? We don't know. We do know that Loro values her friendship with Ramón very highly, and would do nothing to jeopardize it. But I have seen Ramón looking at Loro with something different from just friendship.

I appreciate his wisdom. He knows enough to keep that from her right now, and concentrate on his pre-med studies. Both he and Loro are doing well scholastically. The first year she had to apply herself, and none of us knew if she would make it. But she was able, with Ramón's help, to buckle down and now her GPA is not bad, good enough to get into whatever university she would like to enter.

Did Ramón go into pre-med, hoping to prove himself as a doctor, and win Loro's hand?

Perhaps. But I would like to think that medicine is a calling for him.

As for the Señora, just as I suspected, she has proven that she has a hitherto hidden, but excellent sense of business. As soon as she and Ron got her financial affairs straightened out she put her experience in Cinco de Mayo celebrations to work in beginning a catering and wedding reception business, located at La Fuente which is doing very well. As for our relationship, we have come to love each other dearly. Ron and Tabbie accompany us to church now. Occasionally Loro will go with her mother, and when she was still going to school here, she and Ramón occasionally went with us.

What kind of a churchgoer does Ron make? A good one, although he holds out an option to disagree whenever he so desires. He prays and researches his subjects before he takes a stand. He has told me many times his allegiance is not to the church but to God, and it is God he serves, not the church. I agree with him on this. Churches are organizations run by us poor fallible humans, and, as such, they are subject to human error. When our allegiance is to God, we can tolerate and pray for error in fellow Christians and the church without feeling that we have been betrayed by that error. So many Christians make the mistake of thinking that the church is God, and therefore should be perfect like God. Unhappily, it will never be perfect, so long as its running is in the hands of people.

The Señora's prayer group usually meets at her house now, and I often attend, and Loro would attend sometimes when she was home. I was interested in the fact that Ron has never sought a church office, but when the opportunity came for him to host a men's prayer group he readily agreed. Ramón and his father often attend that prayer group, which is held here at Buenaventura.

I think that it is good that Ron sought a ministry for himself, rather than waiting to be asked to fill a position provided by the church. Often such positions provide a way for Christians to advance socially and prestige-wise. When Jesus said that we are to produce fruit as Christians, He did not lay the responsibility on the church, but on the individual. I think of John the Baptist, who had the opportunity to follow in his father's footsteps and be a Levitical priest in the Temple at Jerusalem, but instead put all that aside, and opted to go to the desert and be a voice in the wilderness. And of Jesus, who had no desire to attain worldly status, but instead turned down worldly status in favor of becoming an itinerate preacher who had no home, "no place to lay his head." The wilderness was their seminary and teacher. Ron's wilderness was his bitter marriage and more bitter single status. In such places, we learn about God and the walk in the Spirit, if we will allow ourselves to be taught.

We spent last Christmas in Alabama with our relatives, and it was wonderful. The Señora went with us, and we met

Loro there. The Señora was delighted to find her daughter in the company of such good people.

However, this Christmas we will spend at Buenaventura because our baby is due in March, and Ron will not allow me to travel so close to that date. I still want the little daughter with black curls, like Tabbie, or a little son with the dark, expressive eyes of his father. Ron said he would take any kind.

But hopes for a baby with turquoise eyes.